Laura Sintija Černiauskaitė was born in Vilnius, Lithuania in 1972. She studied Lithuanian language and literature at Vilnius University and became a journalist and an editor of a children's magazine. In 1993 she won the Lithuanian Writer's Union First Book competition. She is also a playwright and her plays have won awards in Lithuania and Germany.

Breathing into Marble won the EU Prize for Literature in 2009.

Laura Sintija Cerniauskaite

Breathing into Marble

Translated from Lithuanian
by Marija Marcinkute

Noir

First published in Lithuanian as Kvėpavimas į marmurą

Text copyright © Laura Sintija Černiauskaitė
English translation copyright © Marija Marcinkute
The moral rights of the author and translators have been asserted.

Published by Noir Press.
www.noirpress.co.uk
noirpress@hotmail.com

Cover design by Le Dinh Han
Cover photo by Roberto Tumini, sourced from www.unsplash.com

978-0-9955600-0-0

THE FOX'S DEN

He was walking.

The road shone between the fields like the blade of a knife thrust into the west. Shadows rolled over his head and shoulders and the occasional car left steamy tracks through his brain. When he stepped off the road, the grass, which glistened like oil, moistened his shoes. He lived here – like this – between the asphalt and the sky, as if nothing had happened until that moment. The ghosts of the past had been left on the other side of his memory, a niggling, fading noise.

It was as if he had just sprung from someone's imagination; as if he had been shot out above this road through the woods, beneath the weak eye of the sun. The sun's light was undemanding and he floated in it, as complete and light as a speck of dust.

It was as if his purpose was unfolding as he walked.

He moved forward resolutely, unaware, perhaps, of where he was going or why, but deep inside – whatever it was that had been growing in him for years – knew and led him on.

He only had to obey. He had been forgiven everything already.

The sun-baked stones pulsed in the grass. That smell . . . the smell of hot skin. In the evenings when he would press his nose into *her* neck he would sense the hot, anxious pulse of her blood.

'What is it?' she would murmur, her eyes not lifting from her book.

She rarely touched him and he rarely touched her, sensing, somehow, that he was not allowed.

'What's the matter with him?' she would mutter, in the late evening, her voice colourless. 'What does he want?' She was almost asleep.

'Nothing.'

'Well, if you don't want anything, then go to bed. Your brother's asleep already.'

He is not my brother.

He is not my brother because I have no brother. I am unique, born of the air.

A white Porsche slid past quietly as a bowling ball – he remembered having once watched a game on TV. He had also seen a Porsche on TV which you could win if you bought something and filled in a coupon. The Porsche on TV had been red, like the hot water tap in the showers at the orphanage. Long legged girls were wrapped around it like cellophane. They caressed it as if it were alive and as if they had already fallen in love with its winner. It struck him at that moment that love, which everybody was always talking about, was simply about being the way everybody wanted you to be. But nobody could explain exactly how you were supposed to do this. The models who were wrapped like ribbons around the red Porsche had long, slim legs – he had never seen legs like that anywhere else; the girls and women in the orphanage were fatter, with soft bottoms that he was afraid to look at for too long, their legs were solid and their feet were planted firmly on the ground, kicking up a racket as they walked down the corridors. Perhaps the TV models, like an exotic species of hens, had been bred especially to stroke Porsches – or so he had thought as his palm grazed his feverish trouser zip.

The white Porsche slowed to a stop. He sensed immediately it was for him. He pretended not to notice. As he walked past, the front door opened.

'Where are you going? Get in, I'll give you a lift.'

He was afraid – it could be *her*; the light suit, the hair bleached gold by the sun at the temples and the smell – *that* smell, and the foot wrapped in shiny lycra – like her the woman drove without her shoes on – he took in all the detail, just in case. He blushed so violently that for a moment he felt faint. It couldn't be her, even after so many years, and definitely not in a Porsche. And that smell, though it was similar, and the timbre of her voice, and the shiny knuckles like tiny crowns above the wheel – it was all just a clever forgery.

He got in the front, beside the woman.

The car moved off. It drove down the road as smoothly as a knife cutting through butter. The woman asked him a question and he knew he had to lie; about everything – nothing he said should contain a speck of truth. Don't tell them the truth. He didn't know her and didn't want to. At first – when he was younger – it had seemed like the truth was important to them. Actually they didn't really care; they only wanted to know what was most convenient for them. He didn't care what the woman wanted to know – probably just the same as everybody else – some dull, insignificant details, as alike as the alders that grew along the roadside. He was irritated that the woman made him use his brain and waste his breath. He listened to her deep, lazy voice and took his time to answer, noticing how the diagonal rays of the evening sun sifted through the soft, ash-grey hair that rested against her cheekbone. As if sensing this arbitrariness of the light, she took out a pin, let go of the steering wheel and, with a couple of deft moments, skilfully fastened her hair at the back. A velvet shadow appeared in the hollow of her naked cheekbone; a seductive, secret shade – like that on thighs once the lace garter had been removed – he had seen that movement when he was watching TV with the boys. He froze, swallowed thick saliva and squeezed the small knife in his trouser pocket.

'Where do you want me to drop you off?' the woman asked.

'Here.'

'Here? Just here?'

The tone of her voice, her scent and the arrogant arsenal of feminine movements made him mad.

He held the knife to her throat.

'Stop the car!'

Immediately the woman obeyed. She realised he wasn't joking. Without having even seen the knife she immediately understood what lurked at her throat and what it meant.

He just wanted her to understand what he was capable of. Nothing more. He just wanted to see that knowledge in her eyes.

The woman didn't look at him. She stared in front of her at the road which was drowning in shadows. A couple of cars drove by. Simultaneously they both glanced up and then once again he heard the sound of her breathing. No, he saw it throb from beneath the half unbuttoned jacket, from under her linen shirt.

He wanted the woman to touch him, but he didn't know how to say it. How do they say it? What do they do when they want to be touched? Just say it.

Her thin, pale hand on his clothes which stank of cheap washing powder . . . No.

'What are you going to do?' she asked.

She shouldn't have asked.

Because he knew what he wanted to do; it's just that he would never, never have the courage to do it. Instead, he could do something worse. Something she would remember for the rest of her life.

He pressed the knife and a string of blood ran down her neck.

The woman gasped. She began to shake, her eyes closing tightly, her face wrinkling. A moment before it had looked so calm and confident – now it resembled crinkled lace ripped from the thigh.

He swallowed.

'Kneel down!' he demanded.

He didn't want to have to say that – he was ashamed to say it. She should have read his mind and obeyed him without forcing him to humiliate himself. But she couldn't read his mind and he was going to punish her for that. The woman collapsed in a heap on the rubber mat, her breasts pressed against the steering wheel like two small stoats ready to escape, their little faces struggling through the linen shirt, climbing, looking for an exit.

'What do you want?' she whispered.

He didn't know. He just liked holding her under the blade of the knife, liked her whisper, her softness; he could make her do anything, but he couldn't think of what. He was afraid to touch her with his fingers, just the knife, the very point of it. But he could not feel the warmth of her skin. He leaned towards the woman's neck and inhaled, inhaled the fetid scent of the fox's den there – it was *he* who had done it, *he* who had cut open her flesh, *he* who had unlocked the smell. The secret pleasure of the conqueror spilled through him, filling him up to his temples . . .

He let out a long whine, stuck his nose into the cut on her neck and at the same time the tension ejaculated with such force that he nearly passed out.

The woman opened her eyes and gazed out at the road. There was a warm, wet feeling in his trousers; he felt slimy and vulnerable, like a newly conceived embryo. He was so ashamed he felt he could strangle her and stab the road and the woods.

'Whore . . .' he whispered. 'Whore, whore!' he shouted. 'How do I get out?'

The door would not open. Still gazing in front of her, the woman moved reluctantly. There was a dull sound – he shot out and ran under the cover of the low alders, into the dusk of the woods.

He came to his senses only when he reached the fox's den. The one where four years before, holding his breath, he had watched the fox. When he had returned to *her* he had cried and couldn't explain what had happened. The shadows grew longer, the coolness that spread from the cliff breathed on his back, and the wings of the swallows lacerated his chest. His blood pulsed suddenly so heavily and thickly . . .

Unblinking, the fox's hole gazed straight back at him, like an enlarged iris.

It smelt of stale clothes, like in his dreams, nauseous and familiar. Around him the sand pulsed warm, damp and orange. There was no wind. The trees and swallows were silent. His blood stopped throbbing. Only the sand pulsed like feverish brain cells and he dug into it not knowing what he was doing, feeling so small, as if on the way his body had scattered among the cranberries, as if he had slipped off his skin like worn out clothes and left them and soared away. He hurried so as not to be caught or disturbed as he made his offering. The sand was a breathing spirit that was always happy with him; soaking up, anaesthetizing, covering over the paths of his feverish thoughts.

He lay with his knees pressed to his chest, his head stuck in the damp, dark cave, sand grinding between his teeth. When he pulled his head out, he felt the breeze settle like a cool cloth on his face. He had cut his left arm in a few places with the knife – the sand glittered in the small, drying wounds. The same thing had happened at the orphanage. They had even brought a woman in once. She asked him questions, fixing him with a sharp gaze. She kept on asking, not getting angry when he refused to answer. They wanted him to tell them the name of the boy who had sold him the knife. He just sneered.

He found the path easily despite the thickening shadows in the grove of firs. His breath echoed from the arch of the branches returning to him in ghostly shapes. Walking made him hot. It was spitting with rain and warm droplets fell like needles on his nose. He flinched when he saw the light was already on in the kitchen window. His stomach rolled. The other windows were black; they must all be in the kitchen.

Keeping close to the edge of the woods, he circled around towards the small, dilapidated barn. His breathing was so loud that he was frightened when the light went out in the kitchen – had they heard him? But the light jumped to another window – the large room where they used to watch TV and mark books.

They didn't have any cattle. The small barn was used as a store room where the neighbours kept hay – but there was nobody there now. He listened – occasionally rain drops pattered against the roof tiles. There was very little hay; what was there was probably from the previous year, though the dry stems crackled in the twilight, as if they were alive.

Smelling his way to the hay stacks, he dropped down.

He was the only large, dark object there; around him everything else crackled, stabbed and tickled and having been subdued, withdrew.

And perhaps he too wanted to learn how to step away and leave, and for that to be the end of it.

He must have been crying.

Crying for a long, long time in the fragrant, inviting darkness of the barn. The tears immediately soaked away into the hay as if they had never been.

He felt tired and shrunken, like a wrung-out cloth and the last convulsions of his lament trembled through his fingers into the hay.

Then the patter of the rain stopped; it seemed to have cleared up outside and the evening sun seeped through the gaps in the wooden walls. He wasn't sleeping, just hiding in a ball of darkness that was darker than the twilit barn. Slowly, it drained from him like poisoned blood and it was horrible and sweet. He felt its protective radiance, felt how it spread like a pool of urine. He wasn't sleeping, in fact he didn't close his eyes, he was as alert as ever because the darkness required alertness. Then why was it that he didn't hear the footsteps? Grass always rustles when someone walks over it, even someone as quiet and light as *him*.

That boy.

He appeared silently and unexpectedly. The fact that *the boy* noticed him first, stood and stared at him while he was doing God knows what, made him furious. *That boy* had always been like that – *he* always noticed things first, as if, because of some unknown merit, he had the God-given permission to stare like that. He hadn't changed at all, with those bony features that had been sharpened by his illness, looking like a stalk of pale grass. But now they were both the same height.

Surprise drew the two boys into a single, suspicious, trembling unit, but almost immediately a sharp, metallic sound squeezed between them – *he* must have dropped his bike in astonishment. He had probably come for his bike, moved it away from the wall and then noticed him and was struck by surprise.

They shuddered as if halved by the harsh noise and brought back to their own selves.

'Ilyusha!' the boy whispered.

He jumped instinctively. Rage throbbed in his temples. It was as if everything had been preordained and it wasn't even his idea.

It hadn't been his intention.

It was that power that had always been in him.

In the instant before he jumped from the floor, he felt for the knife in his pocket.

He wasn't aware of the movement; he hadn't rehearsed it, but it was as if he had dreamt about it for a long time, in dream after dream, and now it struck like lightning within him. He didn't need to do anything, just step back and allow the force to flow through him, the force which knew better than him and then

that

again

and again

and again

and could it be . . . .

blood splashed the spokes of the bike which glistened in the sun and a black hole steamed in the white shirt,

grass is only pale on the outside, but when you cut it,

such an unexpected colour spills out

its greed and brightness could drive you mad,

how to silence it, how to survive it, if he could have known how it would be

was that him, and what had he done
what had he done
but then
could it have been . . . .
steps crunched across the grass, approaching and suddenly
untamed, ash-grey hair, crackling like hay, spilled through
the sunlit doorway, spilled from fluttering, flowery silk
and then the fluttering collapsed, and everything stopped
those eyes
crystal irises, pistils and stamens flying in smiling
circles . . . they flooded, flooded, steaming
which saw –
and screamed
scrrrrrrrrrrrrrr
scrrrrrrrrrrrrrr . . . .
and so, and so, let me out
it was so tight, it was so bright you could choke, she was
so close
she just
just
having ripped her eyes away from that vivid opening
only then did she recognize him
'Ilya?' she whispered. 'Is it you, Ilya? Ilya? Is it you?'
Her.
Isabel.

TRAPS

HIS EYES were brown, with irises that seemed as thick as steel – they had none of the softness that would be characteristic of a child. When Isabel was taken to the group, they all simultaneously turned towards the door and a hush fell upon them. Isabel froze in the deadly silence, pierced by fifteen pairs of staring eyes. And then a movement rippled out from the corner, a short, slight stir as the boy pressed his tiny fist into his mouth and his eyes flashed. Hardness was probably his most distinctive quality; a grisly toughness. Isabel tottered and stepped backwards, involuntarily, as if she had taken a punch from a stronger opponent; the barely audible drag of her heel across the carpet broke the silence. Somewhere an eye blinked, a crinkle fell out of a shirt crease, a tiny finger moved and, as if a gust of wind had blown through, the afternoon came back to life. But the brown eyed boy stood still at the window, with his sharp, inquisitive gaze fixed upon Isabel. He had something clenched in his small fist.

'Ilyusha, what are holding there? Where did you get that nail from? Don't put it into your mouth!' the nurse barked.

The child didn't move; his narrow pupils drilled into Isabel.

'Ilya, take that nail out of your mouth and give it to me now,' said the nurse.

Ilya's pupils widened, as if he wanted to give the nail to Isabel, but she averted her gaze swiftly to the rug, where long-legged deer were flying, pulling sledges with open mouthed Eskimos swishing their whips. So strange – the rug was brand new and squeaked like newly fallen snow, and for a moment she stood stupidly listening to the sound of its magical squeaks. *Pull yourself together*, she told herself, *what's the matter with you?* She had only to hold the child's gaze. That was all.

When, finally, Isabel plucked up the courage to meet his eyes, Ilya's neck lurched. He hiccupped silently and then his eyes flashed as if nothing had happened.

'Ilya!' the nurse shouted. 'What – have you swallowed it?'

She ran to the child and shook him as if hoping the nail would fall out of him like change from a slot machine. Ilya seemed to be used to this. He shrank and relaxed obediently – as if his soul had already hidden away in some unreachable part in his body.

'Don't shake him . . . he's swallowed it,' Isabel whispered.

Some minutes later she was standing in the headmistress' office and watching nervously as her childhood friend poured coffee into cups with the precision of an alchemist. The thin spout of the coffee pot steamed.

Hearing what had happened, Beatrice Brasiskiene stopped

fiddling with the coffee. Calmly she placed the pot on the tray.

'You told me you wanted a girl,' she said.

'Yes, but now . . .'

'I don't get it, why would you need another boy? And what's more, Ilya Voronovas is not the most suitable choice.'

Isabel nodded in agreement. She knew she would have to listen to Beatrice's counter arguments, that she should keep her peace and then just repeat her decision. She was not bothered either by the fact that *Voronovas' background wasn't clear,* or that *he most probably had gipsy blood in him,* or that *at ten months he had been found in the station so exhausted from starvation and frost that nobody believed he would survive and that this might have affected him psychologically – he had unprovoked aggressive fits.* Or that, finally, *at six, he was too old.*

'Forget about him,' Beatrice said, her tirade over. 'I'll take you to meet the little ones.'

'I want him or none of them,' Isabel countered quietly.

There was such a stubbornness in her tone that Beatrice just held up her hands.

'I found a child for us,' Isabel told Liudas that evening.

'When?'

'At Beatrice's.'

'At Beatrice's? You went to see Beatrice?'

Liudas' pen froze in his hand, the tip digging into the exercise book, the ink spreading in a red pool.

'I want to take you there.'

*　　*　　*

The next morning, as she turned towards the bank Isabel failed to notice a car pulling out of the side street. She waved her arm in the air, desperately seeking a child's hand and stepped back onto the pavement.

'Ilya, how careless we are,' she mumbled to herself, as if the emptiness in her hand would somehow solidify into the brown eyed boy.

Later, she stowed that emptiness in the back seat of her old Golf, among the bags of shopping and an umbrella, and drove back along the snowy road through the woods to the farm in Puskai. That Ilya-shaped-emptiness followed her across the yard in to the house and shrank with repulsion when Isabel bent down to kiss Gailius and enquired, as she always did, if he had remembered to take his medication.

A couple of days later Isabel's car turned once more into the car park at the orphanage. It was two in the afternoon; the snow was melting under the sun, shrinking like a sodden blanket. Isabel was so nervous that it was only when she turned off the engine in front of the office that she noticed she was wearing the wide-legged, colourful, patched cotton trousers she only wore around the house.

What will he think of me? she thought miserably. *I look like a scruffy clown.* She was just about to turn around to go and get changed when Beatrice spotted her through the window. Beatrice smiled and waved, encouraging her to come in.

The electric kettle was gasping. In the air there was the smell of coffee and on a plate there were two cakes with sliced strawberries on top.

'I would like to take him out for a walk,' Isabel said, as she entered the room.

'It's wet,' said Beatrice, doubtfully.

'But it's sunny!'

'He's sleeping.'

'I'll wait.'

They drank coffee and smoked and then brewed some more coffee. Isabel was suspicious that there was some kind of connection between her arrival and the fact that Beatrice was obviously annoyed. Beatrice seemed to be hesitant about letting her see the child – that boy whose face had been hidden among the light folds of her dreams. She wanted to lift the folds and take a closer look at the hidden features of his face, but she couldn't find the words to explain this, either to Liudas or, even more so, to Beatrice.

'Do you remember how Liudas took us to that amusement park once?' Isabel asked suddenly.

She and Liudas had just met; he had come up to her as she was standing by a fountain and started talking to her.

'Excuse me, could you possibly take some books out from the library for me?'

It wasn't so much the nature of the request, coming out of the blue, as it did, that confused Isabel, but rather how good looking the speaker was and how attractive his confidence was. And what was more – there were other girls gathered at the fountain but it was her that he had approached. The library only allowed five books to be borrowed at a time, but the intellectual stranger claimed he had a list of seven he wanted. Isabel agreed to help. It soon became clear that the stranger's request was not as innocent as all that. Isabel borrowed one of the books from him, Henry Miller's 'Tropic of Cancer'. It had sounded exotic. She was drawn in from the first page of the book, though she didn't understand much of it. She was mesmerised by the protagonist's tone and by his sick imagination. But with each page the tone grew cruder and the fantasies more explicit, so that one evening she slammed the book closed with such a smash that it woke up her room-mate. She used to shut the pantry door in the same way when she was a child – slamming it on the rats and other unpleasant creatures which appeared from behind the sacks and the curtains. She never finished the novel and was nervous about what she was going to say if the young man decided he wanted to know what her opinion of it was. She was hesitant therefore about returning it. In the end she lied – all sweaty – that she had lost the Miller and Liudas had to pay the fine. He didn't get angry at all, but Isabel insisted she would cover the expense.

She offered him some money.

Liudas told her to put it away.

Then she invited him out for a glass of wine. He arrived at the riverside rendezvous with a couple of books in his bag. In this way they found the pretext for a series of dates, inspired by guilt and literature. Isabel learnt that Liudas was one year older than she was. He was a student at the Pedagogical Institute, studying language and literature. He, meanwhile, was very impressed that she had been admitted to the Academy of Art that year. For some reason she was ashamed to admit that she had chosen to study graphic design. Neither of them had any idea what they wanted do as a profession and, for the time being, this strengthened the bond between them. Secretly, Isabel wondered what this ultra-masculine, reserved and self-confident man was doing studying in the humanities department. At first she kept an eye out for any strange behaviour that would justify his choice.

There didn't seem, however, to be anything strange about him.

Having struggled through the first chapter of Ulysses – and only stubbornly sticking at it because she wanted to hold up her side of the intellectual discussion – Isabel plucked up the courage to introduce her new acquaintance to Beatrice. She wanted to check what her friend would think about her taste – though as far as men were concerned they never agreed.

Patiently Isabel waited until Liudas had had enough of books and thought of something a little more exciting to do. He suggested going to an amusement park. The suggestion didn't seem to be a particularly romantic one, but when Isabel innocently enquired if she could bring a friend, Liudas seemed to grow suddenly doubtful about what he had been planning. Of course, he agreed. But then he immediately grew upset at his shyness, and felt a fool for letting Isabel keep their relationship on nothing more than a platonic basis.

At the amusement park Beatrice didn't say much, which was strange for her. When Liudas went to buy the tickets and left them under a tree, she didn't say anything, and later, when they were walking back to the hostel at dusk, she was quiet too. They had lied, pretending that they lived on the other side of the campus and were not allowed to invite anybody back to their rooms.

It seemed to Isabel that even though Liudas was her boyfriend – however unclear her rights to him were – he kept glancing at Beatrice and trying to impress her with his humour. Isabel felt the sharp sting of competition. When she was with Beatrice she often felt this sting; it was painful. Occasionally she would provoke it to torture herself.

'You and Liudas took half an hour to convince me to go on that horrible ride. I agreed because I told myself that if I went on it and survived, Liudas would choose me.'

'He had already chosen you by then – have you forgotten?' Beatrice replied. She stubbed out her cigarette and immediately lit another. 'Anyway – how is he?' she asked, her voice indifferent.

'Our little Gailius seems to be stronger this year.'

'And Liudas?'

'Liudas? He's fine, thanks.'

'We're looking for a teacher; one of ours is going on maternity leave.'

'You want Liudas?'

'I think it would be the right place for him.'

They lowered their eyes and lifted their cups, hiding a strange awkwardness.

'Okay, let's go,' Beatrice said finally.

Ilya was sleeping in the far corner by the fish tank with the clown fish. Isabel's dream world trembled and swelled in the sensual breeze – she immediately recognised his short, crow-black hair. From the doorway Beatrice indicated that she approved of what Isabel was doing, and, once she had gone, Isabel, watched by an old nurse, floated along the narrow passage between the beds towards Ilya.

He was lying facing the fish tank with his tiny, sharp nose tucked into the crease of his elbow, having crept from between the sheets like a gift sticking from ripped wrapping paper. His tiny body looked strange even when asleep; it seemed suspicious and ready to jump up any moment and bite. The nurse rustled a packet of biscuits and Isabel jumped like a thief. Ilya opened his eyes suddenly. His gaze was serious, as if he had only been pretending to be asleep.

'Hello, Ilya,' Isabel whispered.

His eyelashes flickered.

'Did I wake you up?'

'*Mama?*'

The child lifted his tousled head, attempting to lean on his elbow, but his hand slid helplessly from the pillow.

'No . . . but I really like you,' Isabel murmured stupidly.

They inspected each other intently without blinking. Isabel smelt the soapy smell of the just woken child – the smell of a healthy boy.

'I saw you.' Ilya's lips barely moved. He was referring perhaps to the day he had swallowed the nail in front of Isabel.

'Would you like to go for a walk with me?' Isabel asked.

'Now?'

'Now.'

'I'm not allowed.'

'The headmistress said you could. Get dressed, I'll wait.'

Isabel expected a friendly gesture, some kind of sign of agreement. Happiness, perhaps. But there was nothing. Just the steely brightness of his dark irises.

'Wait in the corridor or he won't get up,' the nurse whispered.

The nurse had managed to hide the biscuits and appeared silently behind Isabel carrying his clothes. Isabel nodded obediently; she cast a conspiratorial glance at Ilya and then floated back out in the same way she had come in, between the beds with their heavily breathing children.

Ilya got dressed fast. On the landing, at the top of the stairs, Isabel offered him her hand but he sniffed with disgust and loped downstairs.

The sun tore at their eyes. They crossed the deep slush in the car park, blinking, happy that the excessive brightness of the light prevented them from talking. The sun made things easy; it focused their attention on the struggle to see. An unspoken bond grew between the woman and the child as they struggled against the light.

In the woods the sun struck the crowns of the trees and scattered through the branches. Escaping from the brightness, they were confused; they paused and instinctively leant away from each other. They were forced to open their eyes and look round.

Isabel searched for an expression to wear; under his hat Ilya's eyes leapt about, as if he was an animal that could smell danger. Suddenly she saw the soft freshness of Ilya's skin which was like peeled fruit. Seeing that softness a gentle expression slipped across Isabel's face.

'Do you like swings?' she asked quietly.

'No,' Ilya answered. His voice was quiet too.

'Do they have swings here?'

He didn't answer.

'There must be swings. Can you take me to them?'

'I don't want to,' the child muttered, kicking at the crust of snow.

'I do. Let's go.'

They found the swings in the clearing. There was a wooden climbing frame with a straw roof, a skating rink, and a roundabout.

'Hold this.' Isabel stuffed her bag into Ilya's hand and settled on the swing.

She swung up between the sun blotched tree trunks and then back down to the boy waiting on the ground. He shuffled his feet, his eyes fixed on the earth, clutching Isabel's bag as if it were something foreign.

Suddenly he glanced up at her and pulled a face.

'What?' she shouted, short of breath.

'You look stupid,' Ilya mumbled.

'What? What? I can't hear!'

She was suddenly worried that by being careless she had missed something important. She stopped the swing and gazed at the child intensely, as if in apology.

'Open the handbag,' she said. 'There's something in there for *you*.'

There were some chocolate Zephyrs in her bag. Isabel had wandered around the supermarket for a long time before choosing them – Beatrice had told her not to bring anything, so she knew she had to hand Ilya the gift stealthily. She chose something that could be destroyed easily. Tired of circling the pastries section, Isabel had at last spotted the Zephyrs. They were beautifully shiny on the surface and blindingly white inside. She didn't like them herself, but they were perfectly lovely and reminded her of sea shells.

Speechless, Ilya fixed his eyes on the Zephyrs. It occurred to her that this was probably the first time he had been given sweets.

'They're Zephyrs. Sweets.'

Ilya paused and glanced at Isabel angrily, as if she was stopping him from doing something.

'You know what – I won't look. I'll have another go on the swing and you try them, okay?'

Isabel swung so high that the toes of her shoes were level with the lower branches of the pines; as she dropped down through the sun dappled thorn bushes, her eyes shut instinctively.

She closed her eyes against the sun and opened them in the shade.

What am I doing? She thought suddenly. *I'm on the swing trying to show him how to be free and simple. I'm only thinking about myself again.*

Cross with herself, she got off the swing and looked round; Ilya was stood some distance away with his back to her, his head was bent, his hood shining as red as a calf's tongue. A strange anxiety rose in her heart – the child's shoulders were twitching. Briefly he lifted his head and then lowered it again, as if it was too heavy for him and then he cowered down. Against the backdrop of straight, identical tree trunks this repeated movement looked odd and, some-how, sinister.

Isabel flew to him, her feet barely touching the ground.

Bursts of vomit spouted from him. Snarling like a furious fox cub, he drove Isabel away with a rapid movement.

An empty bag smeared with chocolate rustled on the ground.

I shouldn't have left him alone with those damned Zephyrs! Isabel cursed herself and glanced around to check if some-body might have seen them.

She was mesmerised by the spreading pool of chocolate vomit.

The wind flattened the bag against the rough bark of a tree. Isabel leant down to grab it and, as if teasing her, the wind ripped it from her hands. It flew across the snow, lifting and rising into the air. Isabel clapped her hands together and the cellophane wrapper popped and collapsed between her palms; she laughed victoriously, waving the bag at Ilya.

He gaped. That was all. He watched Isabel approach, all sweaty after the chase, wearing a white jumper beneath her unbuttoned coat which looked like a nurse's uniform. Ilya hated white clothes; the people who wore them usually expected something from him, but they were never clear about what it was they wanted.

From a distance Ilya's tiny face was hard and dark, but when Isabel drew closer it stirred like wind-blown blossom.

No, it wasn't blossom yet – more like a tightly folded bud, the petals of his personality firmly knotted still inside, all his lines shy and inarticulate.

Nobody could tell yet when he would bloom, what he would be like and into what he would mature.

One afternoon eight weeks later, Ilya came in to the yard before the orphanage with an imitation leather bag slung over his shoulder. Liudas' Opel Kadett awaited him, glistening in the sun. The children, glued to the windows, watched as Ilya climbed into the car. He settled in the passenger seat with his lips pressed firmly together, next to a woman with a narrow face and ash-blonde hair. Though he sensed the jealous stares, Ilya didn't turn back, or wave to anybody as if he wished a similar happy ending to their lives in the orphanage. At that moment conflicting winds blew through his chest and if he had stopped biting his lips he would have burst into tears or laughter – he was not sure which.

Beatrice kept Liudas behind for some time as he was due to take over the class of the teacher on maternity leave the following week. Isabel and the child were forced to wait for him to come out, as he would, splashing through the slushy snow, joking carelessly like he always did, to drive them out of the yard. Hungry faces pressed against the windows of the orphanage. The fence, though not visible, pressed in on them.

Seeing the picture of a smiling piglet with a ball on Ilya's bag, it occurred to Isabel that she had never seen such a wide smile on Ilya during the two months she had known him. As her thoughts rippled around the child, he shot her a short, eloquent glance and smiled.

And then she could not hold herself back and reached out and stroked his tightly-clenched fist.

Just one light touch, as undemanding as a breath of wind.

The child cowered and stiffened as if ready to run.

'Don't be afraid; I won't touch if it's uncomfortable for you,' Isabel said quietly.

He listened and seemed to understand.

He sat in the car quietly, concentrated, his eyes focused on the office door from where Liudas would emerge. Though his hands remained gripped in fists, they opened slightly, cupping, like the cold, empty glass of a homeless child, glittering in the winter sun, waiting to be filled to the brim.

And so, as February drew to a close, they brought a child with the face of an angry puppy back through the hissing, wet snow to Puskai.

THERE WERE so many dark haired women in the city. The black curls tickled the retinas of his eyes like malicious feathers. He flinched. Nobody noticed because the flinch was hidden deep inside him, deep in his subconscious.

The winter was wild and changeable; the cold was bitter and it snowed. The dampness penetrated the bones like sulfuric acid.

It had been two months already.

Usually they would have agreed a date for their next meeting and he wouldn't jump when a cloud of black curls appeared out of the crowd. Desire would ignite his loins. He would bring her that pent-up desire and give it to her and she would greedily soak up all that he had managed to gather during the hours they had been separated.

Now, when he got out of the car, there was a gnawing in his gut. The feeling of emptiness in his heart was dull and painless, but there were more and more black haired women on the street. The sight of them awakened the old reflex – the emptiness in his heart swelled and then immediately contracted. A reflex spasm. He felt no pain.

He had promised to drop in at the Department for Education and at the pharmacy. He would also go to a couple of bookshops, have lunch somewhere and on the way home do the shopping at the supermarket. They would be angry with him at home for having lunch in town.

He had lunch in town.

Again. Well . . . But . . .

He slammed the car door shut, mechanically pressed the car lock button and crossed the street without look-ing. A figure with pearl-black hair and an ochre wool coat floated past in the crowd; at first the separate parts didn't stick together as a whole in his head – the hair might not have belonged to the coat but if the crowd parted and allowed him to put them together, to join them to each other . . . He slowed down and dug his hands into his coat pockets and for some time the distance between him and the woman with the black curls didn't get any shorter. And then, yes, a warm, dark brown, beaded scarf suddenly joined everything together – at a distance it looked like her shoulders were dripping with molten chocolate.

She was walking rapidly without looking around, just like she always did when she had some goal in mind. When she was at home her footsteps were shorter, softer, enfolded with a graceful laziness. But when she was out, she always walked with a purpose, as if she disapproved of anyone who dawdled or lazed around on the benches under the trees.

Though he didn't feel anything seeing her, he followed her, as if lured on by the light of her curls. His empty heart thudded a little. Just that. He knew that he could stop following her and go back to the car. There he could think.

He could stop at any time.

The curly hair turned off the main road and he began to run so as not to lose her. There she was. There was her dark red Peugeot. And she was sat in it, like a golden seed in a pepper pod.

As always, she had parked her car illegally.

He approached the car on the passenger side and knocked on the window.

She was sitting in the driver's seat fiddling with her bag. Her hair was tousled. Under her feet, on the rubber mat, was a glove and on the empty seat next to her a hastily opened cigarette packet and large silver lighter – a present from her husband.

Her eyelids wrinkled and the lashes fluttered as she slowly raised her troubled gaze.

And then she was looking at him. For the first fraction of a second she stared at him blankly, as at a stranger, and then surprise flushed her face and her red cheeks pearled with confusion.

He opened the door and slipped into the car like a lizard.

They sat for some time, not moving, as if afraid to disturb the silence carelessly. She was the first to turn. When she whispered, her voice barely coloured the air.

'Well, here we go . . .'

He moved slightly but didn't answer. He gazed emptily out of the windscreen in front of him.

'You followed me?' she said.

'I was passing and noticed your car . . . You can't park here, can't you see?'

When she looked at him, her gaze was tortured and terrible.

'It would have happened anyway – sooner or later,' she said.

'What?'

'It would have happened . . . in the street.'

He had thought she was referring to what happened between them.

'I expected that I would bump into you,' she said. 'I was preparing for it. Now, when you knocked on the window, I was ready. Where are my cigarettes?'

He shifted in the seat.

'You're sitting on my cigarettes,' she said calmly, but he didn't move.

'Have you spoken to her?' he asked.

'She came to see me.'

'I know. Was it you who decided to employ me?'

She started the engine and smoothly, confidently, took the wheel and nosed the car onto the main street.

'We needed someone to cover the teacher,' she said calmly, insouciantly, and drove through a red light.

'What are you doing?'

She said nothing , pretending that she was focused on the road.

'Where are we going?'

She didn't reply.

After some moments she said, 'Pass me the cigarettes. They're under you.'

He didn't pass them. He didn't hear her; the request was irrelevant to him. The streets were half empty and they flew along more or less without stopping.

'But why did it have to be me? It's you who thought this up, on purpose,' he said.

And he understood from her silence and from the way she bit her lip that it was true.

'We agreed . . . Do you hear?'

'I do.' She cut him off.

For some time they did not speak. Suburban cottages appeared by the road and trees hovered over them like enormous skeletons.

'Where is your car?' she asked suddenly.

'In the centre.'

'You're on your own?'

'Yes.'

She turned off into the woods and after a couple of hundred metres stopped the car in a slushy clearing next to the river.

'She wants to take one of our children,' she said.

'I know; she's been talking about it for years.'

It was silent. Only the crowns of the pine trees moved as if being tickled.

'These months . . . these last two months?'

'Yes. What about them?' he said.

'They were . . . difficult.'

He took some cigarettes from his pocket and lit one. She watched as the smoke balled, rolling out of his mouth and nostrils.

'You know what I think about that,' he said very quietly, gazing through the windscreen.

'I couldn't care less what you *think*. I can see how you *feel*.'

He cast a swift, sharp glance at her and then stared again at the slow flow of the river.

'Give me a cigarette,' she said, her voice hard. 'Shift your bottom.'

He pulled out the squashed LM packet and offered her one.

'Lighter.'

He extracted the lighter from the same place and their eyes fixed on it as if it were the common enemy.

'Oh,' she said contemptuously.

She bent towards the light, the cigarette trembling between her lips. Suddenly, he opened the car door and with a sharp, angry movement, like the firing of a gun, he threw the lighter towards the pines.

'Liudas,' she whispered.

Her vision dissolved. Tears flowed from her eyes, forcing themselves from between her eyelashes. Liudas shimmered. His face receded and disappeared – and only her gaze was left, swirling and dancing like mercury.

'I'm not asking for anything . . . I just want things to be the way they used to be.'

He took her face and held it between his palms.

'Will you come to work for me?' she asked, trembling.

'I will, Beatrice. I will.'

*   *   *

THE PUSKAI farm had once belonged to Isabel's father, George Jamontas.

He had bought it cheaply from Dionisas Vietusis, a lonely, old, retired teacher and amateur musician. Having paid in cash, her father took a photo of Dionisas in the garden, next to the veranda, which was still in good shape and sparkled in the sun, the colourful panes of glass shimmering like a kaleidoscope. Dionisas had his foot on the step, an accordion on his knee and a newly plucked sprig of lilac stuck in the lapel of his Sunday-best jacket. Suddenly, he remembered his suitcase, so her father had to unlock the boot of the Zaporozhets again, drag out the artificial leather case full of books and photographs and with documental accuracy take the picture once more – Dionisas, lilac, accordion, the porch windows shining like a massive honeycomb beaded with dripping honey and, next to the owner's feet, the suitcase sprinkled with the blossom of the lilac. The mood of the photograph didn't in any way look like a farewell – on the contrary, Dionisas looked like a happy settler, his case stamped with lilac, who had no intention of moving even an inch from the veranda steps.

However, her father closed the camera, offered Dionisas his hand and took him to the yellow Zaporozhets. An hour and a half later the old Puskai owner had signed the agreement which stated that he would stay at an old peoples' home. That was his request – the condition of the sale of the farm. After that, for the next five years, on important holidays, her father would take him a bottle of vodka and would take a picture of him glass in hand, his vital, blazing eyes shrouded by thick, grey eyebrows, an artificial dahlia in his jacket lapel – and, as if by accident, the accordion would happen to be in the shot too.

What Isabel remembered most were the melodies Dionisas played on the accordion and the artificial dahlia. She recalled too the densely rutted wrinkles on his face; a pure carelessness shone from them. Close up he looked as colourful as a lollipop and he smelt like one too. Isabel would wait impatiently for Dionisas to extract from his pocket the carelessness which allowed him to joke and sing, and hoped he would secretly slip it into her hand. It seemed to her that they were all waiting and competing to become heirs to Dionisas' carelessness. But he, though, would sit on the tidily made bed in the care home and lift his glass and happily pose for her father, his smile twitching his wrinkles. He would play his accordion. He was not going to hand anything to anybody.

Isabel could not imagine that Dionisas might die. People like him didn't die. His carelessness would last him for a couple of hundred years.

But early one spring morning the news reached them: Dionisas Vietusis passed away in bed in the old people's home with his best suit on, having failed to leave his carelessness to any offspring.

They had moved to Puskai from the city when Isabel was just beginning to learn to walk and to lispingly ask for the potty. It was there, by the brown tiled stove, that she started to form her syllables 'po-rridge, ri-ver'. At first, when the house was not yet fully inhabitable, the three of them took shelter in the living room. Having hired some men from the village, her father replaced the roof, the floor, patched the walls, enlarged the windows, and built a brick outbuilding with a window in the roof – his workshop.

In the mornings, having washed at the well, half naked, he would straighten up and his beard would flame in the sun.

Her father said that the people from the village were suspicious and slow – they needed time to get used to new settlers, especially those from the city who didn't rear animals and bought their eggs and milk from their neighbours. And they considered the new settlers' garden to be pitiably small; too small to feed a family. When they gathered at the shop the locals would ponder how they made a living. Perhaps, they speculated, money poured from those wooden images the father was carving, like from a golden calf? Her father, having heard about these conversations, scratched his beard and the next time he went to the shop in Kurpiskiai, announced seriously, 'I shook the image and here's the money for cigarettes ... Is that enough, Pranciska?' Pranciska, the shop owner, not having quite the same sense of humour, was not sure whether to laugh or think him mad.

When there were only the two of them left, Isabel began to think that it was her father who had given birth to her – that there had always been just the two of them. He had never known how to make sandwiches neatly because that was how he was – he could carve wooden sculptures neatly but he couldn't cut cheese straight. *That's his nature,* Isabel would explain to her friends, until one of them snapped, *That's because he hasn't had enough practise, it used to be your mama who made the sandwiches.*

*   *   *

She was eleven.

One morning she ran to the barn before it started to rain and the swallows were twittering loudly.

Possibly she had gone to get her bike; her father might have asked her to get some cigarettes from the shop. Or some moonshine. They always had some at the shop; Pranciska would bring it up from the dark pantry, wrapped in newspaper.

The sun was shining as she entered the barn. Later, whenever she recalled that day, everybody said it was cloudy in the morning and in the afternoon it rained. But through the gaps between the planks of the barn walls, needles of sunlight sowed a line across her mother's skirt and her bare feet. Isabel's forehead hit them as she walked in and she jumped. And then she lifted her eyes.

The swallows twittered because they were alive and were full of the desire to live. From that moment on she understood that life should be full of noise – it was life's privilege, its daily battle. Silent things were cold and dark and dangled from the roof beam like an empty sack. Silence was more terrible than noise. It corroded your sanity.

Her father carried Isabel into the house. Later he told her she was screaming and screaming, but Isabel didn't remember that – the screaming. She recalled only a painful buzzing in her temples and thousands and thousands of swallows; the air trembled with them.

Also Isabel remembered the heaviness of the heat, as if she had been filled with hot sand. A dry heat pulsed in her eyes, her mouth and the tips of her fingers; only her forehead tingled from an icy touch. The touch she had brought back from the barn.

Later, like the fingers of a corpse, the tops of the trees interlocked over the slow funeral procession. And the sky felt as if it were everywhere; the easiest thing was to lean her head back and to gaze up into it and allow the gloved hands to lead her. Both her palms squeaked against black leather. They wouldn't let go of Isabel, not for a moment, as if wishing to protect her from the stone that had begun to mutter in her heart. They asked pointless questions, as if trying to drown out the noise of the stone. When the damp, yellow sand thudded like soaked semolina onto the coffin lid, the stone in her heart loosened and rose up and she rose with it.

They carried her away. The low, tepid sky dampened her corneas – she tried not to blink. She dug her nose into the sheepskin collar of the person carrying her; the collar was slippery and pitted like the surface of the moon and she inhaled the man's masculine scent all the way home.

At the house, as a respite from the long black box, a long white table awaited them. Isabel was lowered into a deep, lace covered armchair in the corner of the front room; it stood farthest from all the other furniture and the laid table on which the dishes and cutlery glinted hard and malevolent like a surgeon's instruments ready for an operation. The mourners did not rush back from the cemetery; those who had brought Isabel home stood talking quietly in the yard, outside the open door. She could smell tobacco and hear their soft coughing. With all of her strength she lifted herself from the armchair; it was a kind of rebellion, an act of will, or perhaps a mobilisation of life. It was possible that if she had sat there longer her soul, like a worm of faint smoke, would have left her without disturbing any of those standing in the yard, or indeed the fly buzzing around the lamp, or the shadow of the apple tree trembling on the floor. She was close, so close to letting go that she had to gather all of her remaining strength to pin down her soul within her – and to lean on the arms of the chair with her slim, stem-like wrists and stand . . . To stand up. She stepped across the wooden floor. The fact that she had feet and that she could touch the ground with them distracted her for a moment, but the memory of the legs came back. And then with a quiet, determined confidence in the fact that she was alive, she left the front room where she had been laid by the man with the sheepskin collar, as though she had been just another piece of furniture, or some cutlery. Or their mourning.

In the bedroom, behind the wall, *it* was still there. It was cold, like the drop of a well. Not so long ago a head had rested there. And the sideboard smelled of a cold, drawn-out breath. As sharp as the whistle of the sickle over grass.

No, her mother had never existed. Her father had given birth to Isabel.

What had they done during the winter? It seemed as though there had been no winter; no wading through the snow in the dark to school, no fire burning in the hearth. Early one spring morning Isabel was woken by the snarl of the saw – her father was cutting down the apple trees. She ran out barefoot and screamed above the sound of the saw. Her father turned with a feverish gaze – a terrible, foreign glistering in his eye.

That night he came to Isabel's room for the first time.

He lay down at the edge of her bed with his knees bent to his chest. Isabel woke to the sound of his sobbing; she wanted to turn to him, but her father held her from behind with his arms and legs, a hot arc, breathing into her neck until dawn.

Bit by bit they started to live again.

In the summer a hot wind blew. More and more often her father would return from the village having lost his hat or his shoes; he would slump down on the stone in the yard. Isabel would pour some sun-warmed water onto his bare feet and tell him to sit there until he was dry. In the meantime she would run up through the fir woods to the bridge or even to the village sometimes. Often he had exchanged his shoes for some moonshine. *I've had enough, you'll have to walk barefoot!* How many times did Isabel, with helpless tears in her eyes, have to repeat those words? And soon after she would buy a cheap pair of sandals from the market in town.

At night he would come to Isabel's room and hold her in his hot, tight embrace. At first she thought she had to give in to him; that she had to find a way of leaving that shameful heat behind in the darkness and living as normal as possible in the day light. And yes, as if the night did not exist, in the morning her father would turn into 'dad' and would make his haphazard sandwiches with a whistle. But the night breeze would once again awaken in him that uncontrollable reflex.

At dusk Isabel would be in a hurry to switch on the light.

As she grew older she saved some money and bought a table lamp and put it next to her bed. The cable turned out to be too short and she had to move the bed closer to the wall socket. Isabel slept then in the golden circle of the lamp. Hesitantly her father would wish her good night from the doorway and soon she would hear the squeak of the sofa in the front room where he slept, and then, relieved, she would fall into a dreamless sleep.

But one night the bulb blew and the lamp did not turn on.

Soon after she felt her father's coarse beard tickle the back of her neck.

'Daddy . . .' For the first time she plucked up the courage to speak. She turned around. Her father's face burned from the light of his red beard.

'Forgive me . . . Judita . . .' he whispered. 'Forgive . . . me . . .'

He locked the back of Isabel's head between his palms and turned her to the wall, and groaned into her hair. And slowly his hot grip tightened around her, as if he were wrestling with the darkness.

When her father died, Isabel was at a dance at the local disco being kissed by one of the boys she knew. Later the boy walked her home, all the way along the road as dawn broke, stopping to rest at each bush, or rather so that he could attempt to thrust his hand up under Isabel's Sunday blouse. Each time his hands grew bolder, conquering a larger area and in his hasty scrabbling Isabel's skin began to pulse. She didn't remember the boy's name – just that feeling of the suddenly awakened sensitivity of her skin and how passionately he argued with her, almost begging to touch her. She refused, saying her father would not let her. She did not know then that she would find him in the workshop, in his deep armchair – already cold.

The boy persisted as far as the woods, hoping Isabel would change her mind, but when she ran off, having kissed him on the cheek, the words he shouted after her were like sharp stones. Isabel didn't understand the meaning of the words but his tone hurt her. That autumn the boy was called up to the Soviet army and he faded from her memory, having left in her a scar deeper than kisses.

Light seeped out from the workshop's tiny window. But stranger than this was the shadow the armchair cast on the wooden floor; she noticed it through the window and stopped as if she had been stung. She understood what had happened in her very cells, as if the air had whispered it to her. She had experienced already that silence which spread like dead earth around a body whose soul had departed and which warns you not to come close. Death had drawn its circle and all that lived within it immediately hardened into stone.

Isabel stopped in the darkness, under the apple trees. Around her the night sighed like a river and whispered; the birds chirped and sang, all life looked for each other, multiplied and celebrated.

But in the workshop sat her father in the light of the wall lamp – until dawn, when the nurse who came with the ambulance told her that his heart had stopped about five hours before.

*　　*　　*

ISABEL DID not notice that the snow had melted. One morning, walking to Kurpiskiai, she saw that the road side was blue with violets and her heart squeezed, as if she had overslept and missed something that she would never see again.

'Look, Ilyusha, violets!' she called to the boy trotting behind her.

He muttered something without lifting his eyes.

Ilya would often sink into a peculiar silence, as if a dome had been lowered down over him; a careless word would be enough to cause it. Sometimes they would not be able to put their finger on what it had been. But then, do what they may – caress, talk, cheat, charm him with the latest plastic lions, or ships, or promises, or with the smell of cake fresh from the oven – nothing would move him. There was no melting his silence, not even into anger.

One Saturday Ilya dropped his coffee cup – a pale patch spread across the table and then across his trousers. He gazed at the damp spot as though enchanted but frowned as if in pain, as if the steaming coffee had been his own blood that had spilled out, an odd, pale, hot blood and that oddness was transformed suddenly into a terrible secret. Ilya's cheeks were bathed with hot beads. Isabel and Liudas froze as they watched the child, as if the tears were actual proof that he was alive and sentient. Isabel's hand slid across the table, her movement as calm as she was able – and Ilya did not recoil from her. She rose from her seat and hugged the sobbing child. She whispered into his ear; not words, only meaningless sounds, humming, like the hum of tea boiling. They didn't finish breakfast that day, they moved into the living room crying and groaning – Ilya with his face tucked into Isabel's skirt, mumbling for a solid half hour, his face hid among the pattern of flowers. Later he slept, relaxed and without shuddering. Softly Isabel called out to Liudas and he helped her move the child, who was dizzy from crying, onto the sofa. Ilya settled in a tearful trance; the irises under his swollen eyelids shone like damp velvet. On Isabel's cornflower skirt there was a black patch from his tears, shaped like a wounded dragon.

In the evenings he and Isabel would stay in the kitchen on their own. She sensed that Ilya longed for these moments together. He didn't like asking for anything, or speaking or exchanging words. He would sneak up behind Isabel when she was washing the dishes or reading a book and would stand there breathing down her neck. She would pretend she didn't notice him. Ilya's blood would pound and he would grow suddenly distant and then, embarrassed, he would run to the nursery with the sound of blood pulsing in his ears.

In the spring they would ready themselves for Gailius' epileptic seizures, sensitive to the signs. Luckily that year the signs were late, or perhaps Ilya overshadowed them. Isabel attempted to explain to Ilya what the signs of Gailius' seizures were and told him that he should help his brother if anything happened when the adults were away. Ilya's eyes flashed with anger and disgust.

They never left Gailius on his own anyway, not even when he took the familiar path across the field to the Kurpiskiai primary school. Every day Isabel would accompany him to school and home again along the path which she herself had walked some twenty years before.

'Next year you'll walk to school with your brother,' Isabel would remind Ilya.

The prospect didn't seem to make him happy.

Ilya liked quiet, shady corners. In the evenings when Gailius would settle down to do his homework, Ilya would crouch on the floor in the nursery, where the light from the table lamp did not reach. With his face shrouded by the dark shadows, Ilya would breathe more easily and he would stretch out in the twilight like a black shadow.

Gailius had never met a person who took up so little space. 'It's like Ilya's always trying to become smaller,' he said to Isabel. He behaved as though he was not two but ten years older than his brother. He would not complain to his mother when things began disappearing from the drawers of his desk – pencils and his *tragi-comical everyday reflections* – what he called the pieces of paper with his scribblings on them. Gailius was a little sad about his *reflections* disappearing, though he always memorised them; they were always bubbling away up there in his head, multiplying daily, begging to be scribbled down onto a sheet of paper. He decided to keep the newly written *reflections* in the drawers of his father's desk. Fortunately they didn't disappear from there. Or, perhaps, as the spring matured, they matured too and were not blown away quite so easily.

One morning as it grew warmer, Isabel nearly tripped over Ilya as she hurried into the veranda. He was sleeping on a straw mat, with a coiled blanket pulled from his bed. He looked so helpless; his neck was twisted and a transparent slick of saliva stretched like a cobweb from his parted lips. Damp hair stuck to his temples. Around him, lined up by his childish hand, his toys stood guarding him. Pressed against his chest were his new sport shoes, the ones Liudas had brought from town.

From that day on the veranda was given to him. Liudas brought a folding armchair from the bedroom, removed the empty jars from the cupboard and put Ilya's clothes in their place. From this, the glass eye of the house, the fruit trees in the garden looked like splashes of blood and amber seen through the red and yellow honeycomb shaped window-panes. Ilya would glue himself to the sun-lit glass and disappear; he would not reply if he was called or gently shaken. It seemed that, after that long season in the twilight, the colours mesmerized him.

'They take over him,' Gailius declared.

'Just be happy that he finds something that excites him,' Isabel replied.

'So what? Before you said Ilya was closed in his own little world, but now he's just created a new, more colourful one. If he carries on like this, he'll kill himself with all those colours one day.'

'What are you talking about?' Isabel snapped.

But two month later Ilya was still a stranger to Gailius. Having taken possession of the veranda, Ilya began to use its door to get outside, reducing still further the possibility of him bumping into other members of the family. Isabel felt Ilya was silently grateful for having been offered a place in the free world, but that was all he needed – nothing more. He had no need of help, or attention, or of warmth as would be typical of a child his age. Liudas was content to leave him alone, while Isabel could not settle for this. This small, wild shaman filled her with despair. At first she had hoped the boys would become friends – Gailius was full of good intentions – but Ilya didn't pay any attention to him. When his step-brother approached him he would freeze, as if he couldn't believe it was he who was being addressed. All offers of playing together would fly over his head like a gust of wind – wordlessly Ilya would carry on with the game he was playing or go out to find some more solitary entertainment. The games he played were the kind to be played alone – most of all, of course, if the sun was shining Ilya enjoyed looking out through the stained glass windows in the veranda. He would also spend a lot of time wandering through the nearby woods. At first, fearful of letting him go on his own, Isabel forced Gailius to go with him. Gailius came back later – as pale as a sheet – Ilya had disappeared! He came home just before dinner and from the wicked glint in his eyes it was clear his disappearance had been intentional. Liudas informed him he was grounded. Isabel promised, though, not to interfere with his solitary ways any more.

Liudas was the second most important person to Ilya after Isabel, but he watched him from afar, fearfully, as if Liudas was an unpredictable animal which you could only win the respect of with irreproachable behaviour. What behaviour was expected of him, Ilya had no idea. The large man would take charge in the evenings, his voice a reserved baritone that seemed to hide something; when he came home the house would tighten like a warm fist, while in the daytime it would relax as if without his control things began to loosen. Once, when Liudas was having a wash in the kitchen, Ilya noticed that between the man's legs swung a bag of skin just like the one that dangled between his own legs – only unbelievably bigger. Perhaps that meant the large creature was in some ways the same as him and that it might be possible to win his acceptance.

Twice a week, after his lessons at the Kurpiskiai secondary school, Liudas would get into his Opel and drive to the orphanage. He would get back after dark and though he was very talkative, his features seemed to weaken, to bleed involuntarily from his face, like ripples from a stone dropped in the water.

Isabel did not remember when she started secretly examining Liudas' hands as if looking for blood or dirt beneath his nails. He would drop his briefcase onto the brown leather armchair, leave soapy scuds in the bowl of warm water he washed in and sit at the table gluing models while Isabel cooked the dinner. Isabel didn't ask anything, but Liudas talked enthusiastically about his new pupils at the orphanage, as if he felt it was his duty to share his impressions of the day. The detail, however, would slide away without illuminating the dark hole of the hours they had spent apart.

When was it that Liudas first carried home that new fragrance? Isabel didn't notice it right away. It suddenly occurred to her one evening that for quite some time the whole house had been infused with this new scent.

She didn't do anything to stop it. Silently she watched, resigned, how less and less of him returned home. She watched how he kicked the mud from his shoes as he came in, how he took off his coat and sat down opposite her and talked incessantly, melting slowly before her eyes like a crust of ice at the tail end of winter.

'Mama, when I die, take me to the barn and lay me there,' Gailius said one evening, out of the blue.

He was doing his homework at the kitchen table.

'You'll never die,' Isabel replied, without turning from the stove.

'The barn isn't any use to you anyway . . .'

'For goodness sake!'

'When I try to have a serious conversation, why do you treat me like an idiot?'

'Because you talk like a fool.'

'It's stupid to face the cooker and pretend that your son will live for ever.'

Isabel turned to face him.

'I'm sorry, mama,' Gailius whispered.

'Don't talk to me like that,' she replied quietly.

'What?'

'And don't pretend you can't hear.'

'I can hear everything, mama. I can even hear things that I don't understand.'

'Last night I couldn't get to sleep for a long time and I felt that . . .'

'Did you have a head ache?'

'No, but it seemed that Ilya wasn't sleeping, he was walking around the house . . .'

Isabel was sitting at the kitchen window looking out into

the yard where Liudas was cleaning the soles of his shoes on the grass.

'I think that's what was happening.'

'What?' she asked absentmindedly.

'The veranda door kept squeaking. He walks around at night.'

'He went to the toilet.'

'No.'

Liudas lit a cigarette and stood gazing out at the road, frowning. He exhaled the smoke.

Suddenly she desired him. He looked so distant with his hair ruffled by the wind. That hadn't happened for a long time – that moistness between her thighs when she looked at her husband through the window.

'Ilya's very strange,' Gailius said tapping his spoon on the picture of the pear on the oilcloth covering the table.

Liudas turned towards to house, as if having instinctively sensed Isabel's scrutiny. His glance was terrible. Ignoring Isabel's face at the window which was hot with desire, his gaze pierced the walls of the house like a cold ray of light and then spun back again to the road.

'It seems to me, he'll never be able to be my brother,' Gailius continued. 'And it's not that I don't want him to be. He looks at us like a . . . fox.'

'That's enough!' Isabel interrupted absentmindedly. Having stubbed out his cigarette in a can, Liudas came towards the house.

'You don't listen to me! All the time you're thinking about something else, something a long way away. Or about something that doesn't exist. It seems to me that you're only interested in things that don't exist.'

'You mean illusions?' Isabel glanced at Gailius vaguely. 'Aren't you clever? A fox, did you say? A fox came into the yard?'

'Mama, I think you're all tired of me,' Gailius said suddenly.

'What are you talking about?'

She heard Liudas enter the porch and stamp the mud from his feet.

'I don't understand – why did you bring him here?'

Liudas wasn't in a hurry. There was no sound of his coat being unbuttoned. Just the hum of the thoughts he had brought home with him.

'He's like your spare child. You won't have me for long.'

'A fox, did you say?' Isabel touched her neck; it felt as if it were growing tight, so tight, as if there were somebody standing behind her pulling her gold chain around her throat.

Liudas was standing in the doorway, very still.

'My teacher is afraid of me. When I make a mistake, she explains what I've done wrong as if she felt guilty for having noticed it. She does it because she knows I will not solve problems for much longer.'

'Gailius . . . I'll talk to her. Don't be afraid of the fox. Dad will shoot it.'

Isabel didn't notice when the boy put his spoon down on the table and walked out of the kitchen.

Her legs, silent and light as feathers carried her across to the doorway. Liudas flinched and leaned away from her. He still had his coat on.

'Liudas,' she whispered against his iciness. She suddenly

understood what it was that had slipped away into the twilight.

He saw that she had hit the wall of ice. He felt it, but did nothing.

They stood opposite each other in the darkness. She fingered Liudas' secret. They stood on opposite sides of his coat and held it at the corners as if it were a black flag, wavering for a painful moment.

'Why don't you switch on the light?' he said suddenly, calmly.

'It seems to have blown.'

Isabel pressed the switch and the light burned their eyes reproachfully. They leaned away from each other and, blinking, their eyes returned to normal.

And the dampness between her thighs froze into icy needles, poking painfully at her skin.

There was a scream. It sliced Isabel's throat, flashing like lightning in the darkness over her bed. She woke with a start. The six year old child stood at her bedside gazing down at her.

Isabel switched on the wall light and it flashed like a second silent scream; Ilya ran out through the door as if he had been scolded.

'What's the matter?' Liudas rubbed his eyes.

'Nothing. Go back to sleep. It's Ilya, the lunatic.'

Ilya was crouched in the kitchen, next to the fridge. The look on his face had changed.

She recognised the gaze.

One morning, having taken Gailius to school, she asked Ilya to fetch some wood from the barn. It was the beginning of April and they still needed to light the stove occasionally. Having knelt down by it, she was feeding kindling into the flames when she heard the child's footsteps behind her. She heard the sound of the wood being dropped onto the floor and then suddenly – a sullen silence – and a chill ran down her spine. 'If I had hesitated a moment longer, he could have killed me with his look,' she thought later.

'Ilya,' she had said loudly, not turning around.

He moved, creaked.

'What are you thinking when you stand like that, behind my back?'

'Your jumper has a hole in it,' he said.

'Where?'

'Here.' He put his finger into the ripped seam on her shoulder.

Isabel used to take him to Kurpiskiai and gradually he stopped grumbling and even began to look forward to these outings. The people would talk to him as if he were one of their own, because Isabel was one of their own and he was hers. But that secret gaze, when he thought she didn't see him, when, hypnotised by her daily chores she was inattentive, would cause her to shudder and turn round quizzically, not even trying to pretend she hadn't felt it. Ilya's gaze would flash like a knife hidden in its sheath.

What is he doing to me? She would ask herself, secretly watching him while he ate, or while he was drawing shapes on the windowpane with his finger, or when he would suddenly freeze while fastening his shoelaces as if sinking into the depths of himself. *No, it's not his fault, it's me . . .* But the next day, on her way to Kurpiskiai, she didn't let him walk behind her. 'Come on, you're my friend.' She slapped her thigh, inviting the child to come closer. Reluctantly Ilya caught up with her, but still he walked along the side of the road leaving her the middle.

She tried to talk about it to Liudas, but he just placed his palm on Isabel's forehead as if she had a fever and looked into her face silently. And then once again she smelled the fragrance which made her want to close her eyes and scream.

The fragrance on his palm.

May was stuffy. The air blossomed and the clouds were like translucent petals scorched by the sun which was as ruthlessly hot as a stone hissing in hell. Isabel would get up in the morning already heavy and slide towards evening like a shadow cast by her own swollen body.

Having taken Gailius to school, she stopped by the side of the road above which the dust swirls kicked up by Liudas' car still hung. And the stones inside her grew red with the heat.

Liudas would leave and she would stay, searching the whole day long for somewhere to hide from the monstrous heat.

She would be alone with the drowsy boy sipping milk in the kitchen. He wouldn't wipe the white drips from the oilcloth patterned with pears, nor would he put his cup back into its place when he had rinsed it in the bowl. Later he would slip into the yard or would disappear into the pine woods near the river across the bridge. And moments later she would hear the splash of the stones being thrown into the water.

Isabel preferred to go to the river bank that was at the bottom of the garden, closer to the house. She would descend the slope through the lilac bushes and stop in the shade. In the sun over on the other bank the air would roil slowly and heavily like hot oil. The blossom of the lilac gave off a strong fragrance under the blistering sun. Isabel would pull her old cotton dress off over her head and, keeping to the shade of the bushes, slide into the water. The river would hug her waist tightly at first, then push and pull at her with its mischievous current. The stones within Isabel would hiss and blacken.

The river lashed her skin like a cold wind; it washed away the ashes and rinsed away the names. Isabel would stretch in the water like she was in bed, while the current washed her clean.

On the 22nd of May a fresh wind blew; the grass whispered and the pine forest hummed like a bee hive. Isabel, having gone to put the washing out shuddered and folded her arms across her chest – as if to protect herself from the raging of the trees. But the wind was quicker – it sliced open the old wound and the ache of her heart poured out from her like blood.

She took the boys into the woods.

But with each step her despair grew, sending out branches, an increasingly intricate polyphony of emotions. She would have wept were it not for the boys who pushed each other and ran around. In the clearing Isabel said she needed a rest; she sat on a tree stump and closed her eyes. Through her closed eye lids she watched the wind driven shadows that scuttled around like ghosts. She thought that she would burst into tears but the tough bark around her heart resisted. She dug her nails into her heart as if trying to scratch it out.

She felt no pain – she listened to the crackle of the thawing ice and to the bubble of the coming storm.

It was then that she heard Gailius greet someone. Opening her eyes it took some moments for her to notice a tall, shapely woman – from a distance she looked lighter and softer than the pine trunks. The woman's face was thin and suntanned and her gaze was sharp and pierced Isabel. As Gailius greeted her, she plunged the birch stick she was leaning on into the moss, tossed her knotted grey hair and suddenly a smile lit the dense, quivering network of wrinkles on her face.

'It's my birthday today,' Gailius boasted.

'Oh, I can't ignore such an occasion . . . Give me your palm, I'll tell you your fortune.'

The woman stepped towards Gailius, knelt down and stretched out her hand. Gailius instinctively mirrored her movement. They knelt opposite each other, forehead to forehead, intuitively shielding the fate which rose like steam from the lines on the palms of his hands.

Isabel rose from the tree stump and approached them.

'Gailius, don't do it.' Her whisper was addressed to the woman. The grey-haired crone lifted her eyes, scorching Isabel with a dark gaze.

'Your mother doesn't want us to,' she relented. 'How old are you?'

'Eight.'

The woman was silent. Standing up she smiled at Isabel with the same penetrating smile and strolled across the moss to collect her stick – there was no need for it though; her steps were as firm as her smile.

'I gather herbs,' she explained, turning back suddenly, tapping her canvas bag. She headed back into the depths of the woods and disappeared among the tree trunks as if she had turned into one of them.

'Mama, who was she?' Gailius asked.

'We're going home,' Isabel whispered. Her tone stopped any argument from the boys.

In the evening Liudas brought a cake from town and they all gathered in the garden for a cup of coffee. Gailius had made a card on which he had written his wishes for everybody on the occasion of his birthday. 'Father – I wish that you never run out of petrol half way', or 'Mama – I wish for lots of silk ribbons for your hair'. For Ilya, having drawn a watercolour black bird, he wished, 'Don't be afraid of the light, it only bites at first'.

'What do you mean by that?' Liudas asked.

Gailius shrugged.

They laughed a lot that night; it even seemed to Isabel that she could put up with almost anything – that she could live each day without any expectations and laugh each night without disrupting the daily rhythms of their life, listening to the stories Liudas brought home from town. And she could even believe them. She could stay away from it all, keeping a careless distance.

The moon arose above the woods, a narrow, elegant comma, an eye lash, a tiara. Liudas followed Isabel's look and flashed her a bored smile. And that was it. Immediately everything returned to the way it had been. An owl called in the woods, its dark, velvet sound spread a mournful cape across the heavy, damp soil and the grass which was wet with dew.

On the kitchen table there was a box wrapped with orange paper awaiting Gailius – Isabel stopped short, not knowing what Liudas had chosen and having forgotten, herself, that you were supposed to give presents on birthdays. Gailius blinked and paused. Only once he had run his finger over its shiny surface and it had not turned into anything else did Gailius finally believe that the box was real and belonged to him. He wrapped both arms around it and lifted it carefully from the table – the present wasn't heavy and that disappointed him slightly.

'I want to be on my own when I open it,' Gailius whispered. 'Ilyusha, only you can come with me.'

Ilya loped after him. He opened their bedroom door and let his stepbrother in; Gailius could barely control his excitement. The door slammed and from behind it, moments later, came the sound of paper being ripped. Liudas smiled absent-mindedly. Isabel turned her eyes away.

At that moment there was a scream.

The door opened with a crash and Ilya shot like a bullet into the kitchen. For a moment he hung in the air, his feet barely touching the floor, as if thrown out by an angry gust of wind, then he dashed into the porch and out into the yard, so that only the black back of his head was visible through the kitchen window. The opened box lay on the floor, its glittery glamour gone and though the present was still in it, Gailius seemed to have lost all interest in it. He turned towards the door and hid something behind his back.

'What happened?' Liudas asked.

'Nothing, father . . .'

'What have you got there?'

'Nothing . . .'

Liudas jumped over to Gailius and prised open his fist.

'Something happened to him,' Gailius whispered, holding back the tears.

A wound swelled on his wrist and blood seeped through the bitten skin.

'Ilya!' Liudas howled. 'Ilya!'

Feverishly he turned to Isabel who was frozen in the doorway. She was so pale it looked as if it were her blood that had gathered in the wound on Gailius' wrist.

'Please forgive me,' Isabel whispered and stuffed her fist into her mouth in an attempt to staunch her tears.

'He doesn't get enough attention,' she said, switching off the light.

'I don't give a damn what he doesn't get enough of,' Liudas snapped. 'The child is dangerous.'

'I can't, anymore . . .' Isabel whispered. She wanted to say so much more. She paused hoping he would help her, would start speaking first. But instead he shrank away, as always when she cried.

'Isabel . . .'

'I'm afraid of him. I'm scared to stay with him . . .'

'I told you it would be too difficult,' Liudas mumbled, as

if in apology. The darkness above the bed grew softer; it seemed that he was about to touch her. With his palm.

'I wish you could help more . . .' she said suddenly. And his hand moved away.

'I do what I can,' he said.

The palm, cool now, lay between them, carrying its scent.

The sky above the woods shone like pearl, a reproach to the heavy darkness of the earth. The painfully empty space attracted her. At night, half sleeping in bed, as heavy as a bag of gravel, her body would begin to grow lighter and soon Isabel would feel that if she just rid herself of one last small stone she would rise up into the air.

In the morning, having forgotten where she was going, she stopped half way across the yard and plunged into the pure, sun-filled infinity. Her being seemed to fuse with the sky above her – there was so little left of her within the cage of her skeleton that she seemed merely a smudge in the air. The breeze blew as if it were her own scent, flooding across the land to the woods, to the river, and rising up high – a joyful unravelling of her being.

In the afternoon, while washing the dishes by the well, Isabel froze and gazed at her hands immersed in water.

'I'm going mad.'

Something inside pressed against her temples. It felt as if sharp stones were sizzling in her blood, pressing against her nerves, as if they were moving like parasites towards her heart. They burned and pushed from the inside, as if attempting to push Isabel out of her body. While the stones grew and became more aggressive, Isabel shrivelled and melted.

The thought of them obsessed her; she felt how, with an angry hissing, they multiplied inside her. It was unbearable how they took over her will, her very thoughts.

She grabbed at her throat.

It was cool in the house; it smelt of dry wood. A breeze blew through the open windows. The boys were in the front room. Gailius was writing while Ilya was frozen against the window – dark and hard, as if he might disappear out through the glass into the fields like an invisible kite. It was dangerous for him to stay like that for too long, she thought. One day he'll fly away to where ever it was that his gaze wandered and he won't come back, his body will dry out and crumble to pieces. It will have to be swept up. And that will be that.

It'll have to be swept up, Isabel whispered to herself. 'Ilyusha, come here. Sweep up the crumbs from under the table. And somebody is going to have to peel the potatoes as well.'

Neither of the boys replied.

'Aren't either of you listening to me?' Isabel repeated, louder. 'Ilyusha . . .'

'Leave me alone,' Ilya snapped, quietly.

And then the horror of the stones that had built up inside Isabel was transformed suddenly into rage. She leapt over to the child and hit him across the back of his head.

'What is the matter with you? Why do you hate me? What have I done to you?'

She hit and punched and slapped. She cried in pity and then she was enraged. Her blows stoked up her anger – as if she were trying to hurt herself.

'Mama . . .' Gailius stuttered, lifting his head from his papers.

Ilya cowered and covered his head. He gave in to her aggression as if it didn't surprise him. He did not fight back.

'Daddy!' Gailius shouted through the window. 'Daddy!'

Liudas was cleaning the Opel; he could fiddle with it for ages as if it were some kind of secret door into another world, a magic mirror or crystal ball which revealed a different reality. He had been expecting the shout sooner or later. Preoccupied, he hurried inside, mechanically ripping the dripping rubber gloves from his hands. Isabel was in the same distraught state she had been in six year before when Gailius had his first seizure. It was rare that he saw her like that, but on this occasion he wasn't surprised, or scared, or disgusted. He felt only a lukewarm indifference, like silt moving and rising from the bottom of a pond and settling back down again. He pulled Isabel off Ilya.

'What happened?'

'He answered mama in a rude way,' Gailius explained.

'What did you say to her?' Liudas asked Ilya.

'I told her to leave me alone,' Ilya murmured.

'You'll be punished for this.'

Liudas dragged Isabel out to the kitchen.

'You can't do it like this. It's like you're begging the child to love you.'

'That's because you don't love me,' she whispered.

'What are you talking about?'

'You know what I'm talking about.'

He let go of Isabel without a word and went back out to the car.

Isabel stayed inside until evening, when the darkness had fallen, not allowing the stones to take over her.

Liudas pottered around in the yard at the edge of the woods, down by the river. He did some work in the barn, fixed a wheelbarrow that they didn't use any more, then went to the local shop to buy coffee, and then later – for cigarettes. The boys, on their own, huddled in the corner, or darted from one place to another like shadows. At dusk the air grew cool and hung like moist, healing silk over the skin. The evening shadows blended with the earth like beautiful, smudged paint.

When did they fall asleep? Liudas switched off the TV and, half asleep in bed, called for Isabel. She sat still on the doorstep of the veranda, fading with the light, or perhaps she was sleeping, or dying, or running? She exhaled; a sound that was barely discernible among the others in the darkness – there was as much left of Isabel at that moment as the sound of the mournful lowing of a cow, which barely managing to ruffle the evening silk.

There was the scent of apples in the veranda; the apple trees cast silent shadows against the glass door. Not even a slight breeze disturbed the garden. Ilya was barely breathing. At night his smell grew sweeter; Isabel liked it, this smell of a sleeping child. Quietly she bent over him as if bending over a pot of porridge and inhaled, as if she wished to have a spoon of him.

She knelt close to Ilya, next to this child of whom she knew nothing – disarmed by sleep, his face was barely discernible on the pillow, like an unlocked pantry, the door ajar, an indistinct pale shape in the twilight. She could neither touch nor know him.

Suddenly Ilya opened his eyes, as he had that time in the orphanage when she had come to take him out after his afternoon sleep.

Surprised, both blinked and shrank back. Confusion squeezed itself between them like an *intruder*. But, by holding each other's gaze, slowly the trust grew.

'Who are you?' she whispered. 'What are you to me?'

'I don't know,' Ilya said softly and honestly, his eyes wide open, probably for the first time ever.

'Is it bad for you living with us?'

He thought for a while, as if searching, fearful.

'No . . .'

'Do you ever think about what would happen if you had to go back to the orphanage?'

'I don't want to go back.'

'It's difficult for me with you . . . I'm totally alone,' Isabel whispered.

He seemed to understand. Something shone warm and shyly behind the darkness of his face.

'You need to behave so that you will be allowed to stay – do you understand?'

'Yes.'

Tears ran down their faces. They were not ashamed; it was as if their tears sprang from the same source, a secret glance. They dried their tears immediately, hiding them from any *intruder*, from any ghostly presence that might appear out of the darkness. Their contours softened and sank, blending like whisked milk and the night enfolded the woman who melted into the child and the child who melted into the woman and each into the other.

WEDNESDAYS AND Fridays belonged to Liudas. Beatrice would lock herself in her study and get herself ready. But one Monday morning, hearing steps in the corridor, Beatrice listened, startled – the steps were familiar, but sharper and quicker. Their owner approached Beatrice's office like a bullet aimed at its target.

Isabel!

Her ash coloured hair was fastened up haphazardly and her motley, knitted cardigan slipped down over her sleeveless dress – this was how Isabel had been since she was young, always giving the impression that she was a scatterbrain.

It was as if she still hadn't learned to comb her hair properly and needed somebody to fasten the buttons of her dress.

Isabel blew through the door like a draft, and even when the door slammed behind her, the breeze remained in her ruffled hair and cheeks.

'Hi,' Beatrice said quietly.

'Hi,' Isabel said.

She stared at Beatrice as if this were the first time that she was really seeing her.

Beatrice's hair was as black and smoky as a witch's nest. A man would like to kiss it, to lose himself in its capricious curls.

Beatrice, feeling how Isabel's glance picked through her hair as if searching for evidence, shook her head and indicated for Isabel to take a seat.

'Yes,' Isabel murmured, but she didn't move.

'Well, how are you? How is Ilya?'

'Liudas doesn't tell you?'

'Liudas . . . you know . . . he doesn't say much.'

No, she didn't know. After work he talked a lot. He had always been more talkative than Isabel.

'Isabel . . .' said Beatrice, 'What is the matter?'

'Nothing.'

'Sit down then. Why are you standing up? Would you like a coffee?'

Beatrice was glad of the opportunity to turn away. Isabel's gaze did not leave her as she bustled with the coffee cups and saucers and the shining tea spoons which looked like they had been stolen from a doll's set. *Stolen.* She fixed her gaze on Beatrice's bottom and suddenly felt a painful desire, mingled with loathing for those buttocks squeezed into their black tights; the desire of the woman betrayed, who in attempt to torture herself, wants to experience her husband's pleasures. Beatrice's feverish movements gave off a pungent aroma and the longer she faced the coffee pot, the more the scent became unbearable, the more painfully the buttocks swelled and looked as if they were smeared with oily juices.

Isabel flinched at the smell of the coffee.

A scent can hurt. It can be unbearable. It can torture you until finally you die from exhaustion.

'I won't have a drink . . .' she whispered.

Slowly Beatrice put the coffee pot on the cupboard. She turned around hesitantly.

'What has happened?' She said finally. 'Has Ilya . . . done something? I told you that he . . .'

Isabel felt that if she had a sip of the coffee she would die. She felt that the table was covered with finger prints, that it was contaminating her with foreign memories. She wanted to know what had pressed against its lacquered surface; the prints of body parts, the imprint of whispers, moaning like ghosts, turning into reflections on the dark, lacquered surface.

'Take a seat, for goodness' sake.' Beatrice's patience snapped and Isabel sat obediently on the edge of the chair.

Isabel's features seemed to have melted, as if they had been washed away by the current; only a nervous tick tugged still at the corner of her lips. Beatrice knew that she would never allow herself to show that kind of vulnerability in front of Isabel. Not in front of anybody. With a sudden feeling of superiority, she began to pity to her friend. Temporarily emboldened, she braved Isabel's gaze, toying absently with a white, encrusted gold bracelet on her wrist.

'Nice.' Isabel had noticed it.

'What?'

'Liudas likes white gold.'

'Oh,' Beatrice replied coldly. She wanted to turn away. Isabel's eyes were fixed on the bracelet, as if she were trying to decode a text hidden in the tiny amethysts.

'It doesn't suit you,' Isabel said.

'You can have it if you want.'

'Go to hell, Beatrice.'

'Oh, our coffee,' Beatrice exclaimed naturally, as if she hadn't heard.

It was true that she had left the coffee on the table top and it provided a perfect pretext for Beatrice to turn away. She brought the steaming cup over to Isabel, taking her time to find the sugar and then a tea spoon. She felt that something had weakened in Isabel's gaze; it had slipped away, got lost.

'How can I carry on living?' Isabel whispered her anger dissipating.

It was as if she were begging to have her hand held on a fairground ride which was about to shoot her up into the sky incredibly fast.

'Does he love you?' Isabel asked.

Beatrice placed the sugar pot on the table and slid the cup of coffee towards Isabel wordlessly.

And then she jumped – Isabel knocked the cup from the table.

She's insane.

The cup of white coffee pooled on the carpet forming a tiny skull-like shape.

'I said I didn't want a drink,' Isabel breathed.

She jumped up, her hands pressed to her chest as if afraid that the beast encaged within her rib cage would escape. Hastily she ran with it to the door.

'Women are so cruel,' she said, turning suddenly. 'Especially former friends.'

'Just stop it . . . You're turning into your mother,' Beatrice snapped back.

Isabel didn't answer. She closed the door quietly, as if the noise might harm her. Her steps faded down the corridor like the nervous pulse of a weakened heart. Beatrice lit a cigarette. She wanted to call out, but only managed to throw her hands up into the air – her palm thumped down on the table and opened up helplessly.

She began to cry. She looked down at her polished nails
– when she was a child it had been enough to wet them
with her saliva and stick chamomile petals on them and
she would turn into a princess. Beatrice would always
manage to keep them on longer than Isabel – *Your saliva is
stickier*, Isabel would tell her. The velvet petals would peel
from Isabel's first hand while she was sticking them to the
other.

Beatrice gazed at her upturned hands and did not recognise them.

Her fingers lay half open as if pleading for the strength to
pray.

ILYA WAS not at all surprised when they told him he would
have to go back to the orphanage. It seemed as though he
had been expecting it all along.

Isabel persuaded Liudas to call Beatrice and explain everything – but she couldn't clearly formulate what exactly it was
that he should explain. The words scratched around her
mind like mad dogs biting each other and then, finally,
having failed to find any other escape, they spread through
her body in a nervous tremor. Liudas attempted to calm her
with his palm, but his touch was as cold as a doctor's and
together with the trembling it killed something more in
Isabel.

'I visited Beatrice,' she said suddenly, unexpectedly – he
had only asked her if she knew where the axe was. Liudas
froze, standing with his back to her at the little sink on the
wall; he might have been washing his hands or perhaps he
was just thinking about something.

'So what?' he muttered. 'So maybe I don't need to call her?'

'We didn't speak about the child.'

'Look, don't start stressing me, Isabel,' Liudas snapped back, his voice dry.

He went out to get the axe. He hadn't, in fact, been planning to go out when he was standing next to the sink, but now he went. Isabel had no other means of revenge other than to pour out her anger on Liudas' head. He didn't protest.

It was left up to him to think of what to say to Beatrice. He kept postponing the call until it became absurd. When, finally, he managed to dial the number, Isabel's ears began to ring – they rang terribly. Understandably, Beatrice was annoyed. Isabel turned around and closed herself in the kitchen, just in case she could still hear through the terrible ringing in her ears how Liudas attempted to keep his tone neutral as Beatrice reproached him; *she had made concessions for them, they had managed to get her into trouble, she was risking her job and reputation. Isabel, on the other hand, Isabel lacked any kind of responsibility and it might be a good idea for her to be adopted* . . . Liudas managed to cool Beatrice down quite quickly. They made arrangements for the following week. Having put the receiver down, he circled Isabel as if she were a table or a chair, which meant he was still angry and disappointed and not yet sure what his opinion was about it all. Ilya had to be sorted out and it was clear, though left unsaid, that this too would be Liudas' responsibility. Isabel only gave in about one thing – she agreed to sit with Liudas and not to argue with his decisions.

*　　　*　　　*

The next week Isabel stood among the fir trees, her hands crossed upon her chest – the paleness of her hands shone from a distance among the tree trunks. Liudas, in the yard by his Opel, felt her presence behind his back. Gailius had wanted to go with Liudas and Ilya. He looked unwell and Isabel had been worried that there could be another seizure coming. She had begun to argue with Liudas, but even though Liudas was ready to give in, she suddenly lost any strength for the fight. *Just go.* Ilya had squeezed himself in the corner between the sink and the cupboards and, with his irises like steel pins, stabbed at Isabel. It seemed to her that he was angry about that night in the veranda when they had cried for each other; it had been a peace offering, a contract of mutual responsibility, irrevocable. Isabel could not hold his gaze. She turned away quickly, pressed her fist to her chest and unravelled, like thread from the spool, towards the woods.

She didn't hear the sound of footsteps in the yard, or the movements which had sparked the sounds. She listened to the soothing sigh of the fir trees at the edge of the misty woods; the sigh blew through her mind like a cool wind. And that was it. There were no other thoughts. She imagined being small, as small as the comma shaped ray of sunlight shining through the pine needles onto the moss – but the more she tried to diminish herself, the stronger the pressure grew in her temples. She stared at the quivering arabesque of sunlight in the hope that it would redeem her. She longed to burn, to be consumed, to be released from the necessity of standing like that hearing nothing.

The yard had grown quiet; no footsteps echoed. Liudas shouted to the children. She didn't catch the meaning of the words, just the angry scratch of the shouted words frozen in the air; the tone tore at the meaning – and Isabel attempted to turn herself into nothing more than the quivering ray of sunlight. First the car boot slammed, then twice the sound of the doors shutting. Liudas started the engine. She closed her eyes and inhaled.

That's all, that's all. That's all – the words pulsed in her temples. The car turned out of the yard and faded away into the distance.

And suddenly, right beside her, as if having slipped past the guards, a high pitched coo-coo. Coo-coo, right at her temple, coo-coo. Time moved into its painful current again. Coo-coo, a storm arose in Isabel's chest – first her eyes darkened and then suddenly, sharply she fell onto the moss . . . She leaned back against the trunk of the fir tree. A spasm contracted her to the size of a nut and then suddenly she expanded again and she pulsed like this, within the eternal now of a sob, while an occasional scream struck like lightening. And then she listened to herself – the sob expanded into a long, sharp scream which pierced the beams of sunlight – it was cerulean and fast, it shone like lightening above the woods and it no longer belonged to Isabel; she belonged to it.

She had not noticed that she had fallen onto the moss. It was warm and soft and familiar. And quiet, and light, and forgave everything. Here the patches of sunlight moved slowly, promising to return, to repeat. Isabel hid her face between her knees and bit into the flesh of her fist.

Until dusk.

*   *   *

That night they went to bed late, just the three of them now. First Isabel lay down in the children's room next to Gailius who was already half sleeping on his back, face towards to door, as if he had been expecting her. When Isabel lay down next to him, he murmured sleepily without opening his eyes.

'Thanks, I don't need a bed-time story anymore.'

'Are you angry?' Isabel asked.

'No. Why should I be?'

'Well, for all this . . .'

'I just find it difficult to understand you,' Gailius sighed. And turned his head towards the wall.

They said no more. An exhausted despair spread like poison through her limbs and she closed her eyes. Isabel slept, then woke as if shaken, though nobody had touched her. Next to her, Gailius was breathing deeply and rhythmically. She was flooded with a painful feeling of gentleness; in the moonlight the contour of his jaw shone, his scent was softened by sleep. Since his first seizures, when he had begun taking medication, sleep had covered Gailius like a flag of distress. The scent reminded Isabel of the transience of motherhood and of her own mortality. She wanted to touch the florescent jaw of her son, which looked as sharp as a grave stone. The rest of him was lost in the darkness of the sheets, as if only this frighteningly blue and perfect crescent moon shape was all that was left of her child. She touched it with her finger tips; his skin burnt them with its coldness, perhaps because of the other worldly light. Isabel removed her hand and screamed in her head. From his frozen lips she heard the quiet sound of an asthmatic ch ch ch.

When she touched him again, everything was back to normal. It left her with a feeling of sorrow, a premonition, the wisp of her imagination, a heart swelling up somewhere on the shores of consciousness. Gailius sighed in his sleep and she felt, for the thousandth time, that she was losing him. It was like observing him in his agony down at the bottom of a bottomless well. How could she leave him alone under those cold sheets, with the malevolent light from the window stabbing him? She knew Liudas wouldn't be happy, but she felt like bringing her blanket and laying down next to Gailius, on the other bed which was empty now.

In her bedroom Isabel sat on the bed in the darkness. She wanted to say something; she felt that Liudas was awake. The house enclosed them like a dark womb, moaning and sobbing, but Liudas' back was silent. Deliberately silent.

Suddenly she jumped at the sharp trill of a nightingale – it was so close, as if the bird had landed by her ear drum and stabbed her brain with the hot needle of its song. Startled she suddenly recalled a dream she had had a couple of nights before – Liudas' face wobbled on the body of a crane, distorted terribly. A beak forced itself out of his face, too large to be that of a bird and at the corners of his eyes two bloody berries coagulated. Isabel was also a bird. They lay, beaks together, in the warmth of a nest made of moss and twigs, close to the water; they were looking into each other's quivering eyes and plucking at the umbilical cord of despair that joined them – their only pulsing creation. Liudas was determined to destroy the hieroglyph of their two dying bodies, repeatedly lifting his head on his trembling neck.

His gaze did not shift from Isabel. His head flopped hopelessly and, as he pecked at the moss, his irises would contract suddenly to the size of the eye of a needle.

That was the dream.

Isabel stood up and crossed bare foot to the window. Liudas moved, listening – so he wasn't sleeping. His thoughts were too loud and too fast and by trying to control them he had exhausted himself and couldn't sleep.

The night flooded in through the window, as soft and slick as a raven's feather. It smelled of damp soil and excited the senses. Here, at this window, Isabel had stood ten years before, trembling and as juicy as an overripe cherry.

It had been in the afternoon, her father already dead, when she brought Liudas into her empty house for the first time. Isabel was standing by the window and *could feel the air quivering in the heat and heard how the uncut grass rustled in the sun. From deep within a silent nectar oozed from Isabel. Liudas leant against her back, lifted her dress and parted her buttocks and there, even more secretly, the silk ripped. Down her thighs rippled waves of excitement. The honey stirred, rippled and oozed. Her honeycombs bubbled and yielded as she allowed him to take her.*

Pranciska had been driving her goats along the edge of the woods. She waved at them lazily as she hurried the animals along with a stick; Isabel and Liudas waved back, restraining for a moment the trembling of their loins.

And then – then there was only the wind in the grass in the yard and a faster breathing, the silent trail of the plane in the sky which soon would fall behind the shawl of the apple tree, there was only the wood of the windowsill which pulsed and the

alder trees which were ruffled by the breath of the hot wind.
And they were both quiet for a second, before the explosion
which was rising already from within their cells . . . . . . and
then a sudden dive . . . .
And a fainting throb spread through the tissue . . . .
A dive . . . . . .
And a mouth open like a shell as it spits out the pearl . . . . .
A dive . . . .
And the heavenly cork shot out and rose with a whistle, their
howling bones vibrating to the frequency of the light and then
the waning into one another . . . .
and then . . . .
the deathly ball rolled forward with a tremendous speed along
the corridors of bliss . . . .

Isabel stepped back from the window. The bed creaked in
Gailius' room and she remembered that she had decided to
sleep with him that night. She felt then, suddenly, her desire
rising, dark and thick, as it is when it is brought on by
despair. Liudas lay silently; quieter than someone who is
sleeping. She approached him, willing him to feel her desire;
the darkness glowed like hot coal. Liudas did not make the
slightest movement to give himself away.

'Liudas . . .' Isabel bent over him, flaming, touched him
with her smouldering hair and nipples which were as hard as
shards of coal. Liudas moved and mumbled, 'Let's sleep.'

Isabel leant back. The darkness cooled immediately and
tightened about her throat like an icy noose.

'Isabel?' Liudas lifted his head. 'Where are you?'

'If you are planning to leave . . . go now,' Isabel whispered
from the doorway.

She plunged out into the tepid summer night – later she would recall that feeling often – that was probably how a man plunges into a woman's womb. She shattered like a glass broken, in a moment and to her very depths, and, feeling barely heavier than the air itself, felt herself scatter across the yard.

At dawn she found herself in the fields, naked, with her nightgown bundled up at her chest. When dawn broke it was warm, not painful; it was like a careful hand pulling a dressing that was stuck to a wound. The light returned Isabel to her body; she shuddered suddenly from cold and from the weariness in her loins. She pulled on her night gown and took herself home, shivering.

A grey light seeped into the bedroom. Liudas was breathing evenly, lying on his back; sleep made his features look even colder. She was in no state to go back to her child; she barely remembered she had one. She remembered nothing about the things around her, except for the armchair and the early sun light falling through the kitchen window onto the floor. She wrapped a cover around herself and settled in the kitchen, on the same armchair she had been lowered into during her mother's funeral by the relative in the coat with a sheep skin collar. After her father's death she had moved the chair to the kitchen and put a bag of sawdust under its missing leg.

Isabel placed her cheek against the back of the chair and gazed at the sliver of sunlight moving barely perceptibly across the floor boards. She travelled with it, as if riding a pony trimmed with ribbons under the lime trees in Vilnius, across the park which shook from the blare of trumpets. The pony knew where it was going to take her, she trusted it. She trusted it implicitly. Her thighs were warm from the pony and a little sore – it was no joke straddling it. The crowns of the lime trees rustled like sweet wrappers and Isabel's eyes were glued to them. Early autumn sunlight shone through the leaves, as if through a green tapestry.

In the morning Liudas left for town and didn't return.

THREE

THE DOOR to the barn stood wide open, a stone stopping it from closing.

Light from a murky sunset fell through the open door onto the floor. Deeper into the barn the skeleton of a bicycle sparkled in the sunlight. And then she saw, and in that fraction of a second before her eyes had adjusted to the dusky light, understood what she saw.

She leapt forward,

and then there was nothing of her left, just her son lying like a shadow, flat on the earth.

She had seen him like that many times before – like *that* – looking as if his blood were mouldy and shining through his skin – green inclusions in the blood vessels at his temples. So many times before she had seen his face heavy and pure as if it were made of antique marble. Perhaps that was why she wasn't surprised, having had all those times to rehearse for *this* moment. And there, below the face, lower, in her child's stomach, flamed the bloody jaws of hell illuminated by the evening light falling through the door. It was impossible to resist the blood; it called out from the body's deepest mines – it screamed directly to her own blood. Her blood howled, as if it were her not the child that was wounded, it rose up to spurt out of her, struggling to find an exit.

'Ilya!'

His eyes – the steel irises and the black pinprick of his pupils – were not the same as before; their darkness was diluted. They cried and pleaded for something Isabel couldn't give. He held his fist at his thigh, strangely, as if his arm had just sprouted out of his body and he had no idea what to do with it.

Something glistened and quivered in his fist. A knife.

He stood immobile, the knife's bloody tip pointed like an arrow at her son's wound.

Isabel hesitated and drew in a deep breath; the sound seemed to nail Ilya to the wall. The knife dropped to the floor. He squirmed and slid along the wall, his back shaving the planks. She knew what he intended to do immediately – as clearly as if she had put the idea into his head herself.

She blocked his way, grabbed him by his throat. She lifted him up and pressed him against the wall.

She looked not into his eyes, but at the yellow chin that had grown larger over the last four years. He pressed his palms against her face. With the click of a lock springing open, she felt then, with the pure force of parturition, that she could strangle him, but just as she lost all restraint the *call of the sacrifice on the floor* broke over her. She pushed Ilya away; she tossed him towards the door through which the evening sunlight fell. He, a light, tight knot of fear, slithered away into the grass towards the wood's edge.

The crunch of his disappearing steps echoed in her temples,

as she turned back.

Her child was so big on that barn floor. Too big to be scooped up. Only his head was small, with its face growing heavier, like a thimble stuffed with gypsum – much smaller than the steaming nest in his gut. For several long moments she still hoped to sort it all out, to draw him to her like some knitting and hold him until everything in him grew together again, till everything healed and began working.

She pressed the child's face between her palms as if trying to staunch the steaming life that was flowing out of him. She slapped his cheeks in attempt to shake out a sigh or a sound, but he did not respond to her touch. His features grew strange. They folded up, like blossom shrinking back into its bud, and it seemed to her that she was watching her child from the window of a train that was moving away. She looked and could not do anything more.

Still she tried to hold him. She tried to lift him, or thought about carrying him, but the jaws in his stomach bubbled threateningly and she could do nothing but give in to hopelessness. That was all.

There was a mobile phone somewhere in the house.

She walked out into the light with a peculiar slowness. As she forced herself along the path through the grass towards the house, the light pressed around her like glass armour. They never knew where the mobile phone was. She ran from room to room, lost herself at the sideboard, pulled herself back together at the bookshelf with a calendar and finally pulled out, from under a pile of newspapers, the old Nokia. She pressed the keys. Spoke.

Her voice sounded as though it came from somewhere beside her, to the left, as if through a loudspeaker.

Twice they asked her to repeat what had happened. She grew confused. She couldn't find the words, because they were just not there. The woman at the other end of the line was casual and seemed, at first, annoyed. Only once she had checked the details did she relent suddenly, seeming finally to have understood what had happened. It had been a long time since Isabel had last had to call an ambulance, or perhaps the woman was new; she didn't know the way to Puskai and thought the driver might not know either and Isabel patiently explained, a couple of times, where the ambulance should turn in. *'Have you called the police?'* the woman asked. *The police. Call the police.* The woman wasn't in a hurry. She wrote down her notes as the line began to break up; her pauses were like wounds through which the child's life poured away. Perhaps each moment was still crucial. The woman didn't seem to understand this, she said: *I have to write it down, don't interfere with my work.*

Isabel cut off the connection and, stumbling slightly, turned to the window. Somebody moved in the dark doorway of the barn and the bright reflection of the grass was so sharp it made her sick. A blue checked shirt scooted along the wall of the barn towards to woods.

He had gone back for his knife.

And then her focus returned. She leapt out into the yard; her feet were like spears pressing out the fatty sap from the soil. The woods started behind the barn; the blue checked shirt jumped still among the tree trunks. The woods belonged to Isabel, she was faster there; the trees gave way to her and the moss pushed her forward. She did not need to go round the shrubs or bushes. Her face sharpened, transformed into the beak of an eagle. Soon she would catch the runner.

The ferns stuck to Ilya's feet; he grew tired and slowed down. Isabel grabbed him by the shoulder, turned him to her and pushed him down to the ground. Their weight pressed down the ferns which stank of the child's fear and desperation. As she was about to dig her nails into the child, a glance flashed between them.

The glance invited closeness and silence. And this they found.

Everything stood still.

They gazed at one another. In Ilya's pupils she saw the contours of her own face reflected and she was frightened by the sudden thought that she was gripping herself. Her rage evaporated and she slouched down strangely.

Ilya's yellowish eyes were like bursting buds; tears rimmed the whites, one slight movement and a wet trickle ran down his temple. She did not recognise his face. Not the features, but what shone through them; the wrinkles and twitches, like a foetus ripped from the womb. His face had never been so open and helpless, making her want to shade it from the light, to sew it up, bandage it. As if she was looking not at cheek bones and eyes but at the exposed brain. And it hurt to look at it. *Let me go, let me go, missus, I won't do it again.*

She let him go.

For a couple of seconds the child lay still, not believing it was over.

It was not him that she was looking at. Rather, she saw herself; how she would have to rise up out of the ferns and make her way back there, to sort things out *on her own*. She stepped away from Ilya and he jumped up, suddenly, like an animal released from a trap and, without a word, disappeared into the ferns. She did not look; she heard the sound of him running. In her ears, along with the sound of the boy's feet, a silent stain spread, drowning out everything.

She stopped in the middle of the yard, halfway between the barn and the farmhouse, her heart sensing the door's gaping mouth. That was as far as she could manage. From the darkness of the barn something was spreading that was stronger than her and it held her there, preventing her from moving.

The darkness flooded around her, but it had no weight or pressure. It gathered Isabel and held her, gently rocking her until the *ambulance*, white as a ghost, appeared from the woods.

OFFERINGS

A SKYSCRAPER glittered in the dusk on the other side of the river; cars were strung like a festive garland as they crept across the bridge. It wasn't a holiday, just an ordinary working day. Downstairs, people were moving about, looking forward to a warm dinner and an evening in bed watching a film. He sat smoking in the darkness, exhaling through the gap in the window. In the skyscraper across the river there was a darkened window; half an hour or so ago the light was on – today, again, he had been the last to leave the office of the 'Liudvikas' travel agency. When, in the lift, he remembered he had forgotten to switch off the lights, he had to go back again.

'Have you noticed how the days are getting shorter?' his new secretary had said towards the end of the day. It was true. In the summer the computers were the only thing consuming the electricity; they would walk out of the office into the sun lit streets not having had to switch any light on during the day. Now he had to get used to electric lighting again – it saddened him and filled him with the kind of heaviness grass feels anticipating autumn.

He bought some donuts and mineral water at the ground floor café, then, lighting a cigarette, he crossed the bridge; he almost bought another copy of the newspaper which his secretary had left on his desk that morning.

At the bus stop a gipsy was hanging around, as she had been the previous day. When he crossed the road he knew she would say something. He pushed his hands into his pockets, quickened his pace and ducked past her with his eyes down. Back in his flat he lit another cigarette. He paced the dusk darkened room, greedily inhaling the tobacco. He could not get the gipsy's quiet, sharp words out of his head. He hadn't caught the meaning, but he felt as if she had seductively flashed her breasts at him.

When he got home he didn't feel like switching the light on. He hadn't got round to buying curtains. 'Don't you have anything to hide?' his secretory mocked him gently. When she stayed behind doing overtime, the secretary could see from across the river how he came home, switched on the light and smoked, aimlessly pacing his room.

'There's nothing to hide,' he answered. 'I'm as empty as my living room.'

The living room, it was true, was quite empty. Its walls were painted white. On one of the walls there was a Venetian mask covered in glitter, which had been left by a woman as a gift. This solitary decoration would often depress him but he never got round to taking it down, though there was nothing particular he wished to remember about the women who had given it. Disconnected as it was from any memories of his past, it did, in a strange way, fit there – matching perhaps not the walls but rather the emptiness. It was a mirror to his invisible grimace.

He put the kettle on and took a bite out of the greasy donut. It wasn't fresh. He threw it on the table and lit another cigarette. The light from the street lamp fell through the archway into the other room, where he kept his clothes and books. He had never slept or worked there, except for a few times when guests had stayed the night.

Behind the other wall his son's room throbbed with emptiness. When it had been decided that his son would attend the secondary school in town, he had bought venetian blinds for the room straight away. The glass door to the room was black in the dusk, like an enormous block of chocolate. When his son was away, he kept the door closed.

He was left with only a spacious, half-empty room where there was a cooker, a cupboard, a writing desk on which he had his meals and did his writing and a fake-leather, light, brown sofa in the centre of the room. This was where he slept, read or battled for hours with the blocks of ice in his head – during the night they would rise up to the surface and scrape painfully against his temples. Buried deep within the ice was a question that niggled at him, which shouted and begged him – something needed to thaw. But he refused to listen. With an enormous act of will he would push the blocks of ice back to the outskirts of his conscience. To fortify himself he would pour a whiskey.

That was how he passed the hours.

He made some strong tea. As he reached up for the packet of tea some medicine fell out – he always had it, just in case.

He picked the medicine up from the floor and placed it back behind the tea and coffee. And then he lit another cigarette.

The phone was silent. He knew he could call first but he was afraid she would be next to him and that would make the child nervous; they had agreed that the boy would ring. He had bought him a mobile phone; it was a used one, so it didn't matter if someone took it from him. His son looked like the kind of boy you would itch to take something away from.

He went over to the window and blew smoke through the gap. From somewhere below drifted the sound of an operetta; a piece by Puccini. Suddenly he regretted that he hadn't bought a music centre for his son. The boy had lingered over one, but couldn't pluck up courage to ask for it. He knew his son needed music to replace the sound of the trees which were sparse here in the city; the trees grew meekly, subdued by the noise of the city. The wind couldn't get them to talk. He liked his son's taste in music, but music, like electric lights, filled him with a longing he didn't want to think about. He only ever switched the radio on for the news. When he employed a girl he would warn her that he didn't like music in the office.

The gipsy was still out in the street. She was circling around lazily and seductively. A car would stop sooner or later. He wondered who these people were and how it was that they had come to this. The gipsy had hair similar to that of a woman who used to intoxicate him. She had a seductive dimple in her cheek which promised to take you to the sweetest, most fulfilling places, but never took you anywhere. He knew how it would all end. To be more exact, how it would never end – the misery and helplessness, the stupid inability to drop it all. To give up hope. Repeatedly, now, he blew cords of smoke down from the window as if he wished to bind the gipsy to the post of the bus stop. In his mind's eye he waited there together with her. He imagined what she was like when she was with a client and what she was like later, back at home in a hut with no running water, with cockroaches rustling beneath the wall paper and babies murmuring in their sleep. She looked ageless; like a teenager matured too early through drink and men, with a tough but exciting body. Looking at her body he imagined her babies, like roasted sunflower seeds, all similar to each other. When the gipsy saw him with his hands in his pockets as he crossed the street, it was like she could see through him – could see the bare walls of his apartment with the Venetian mask and his son's medicine that dropped out of his cupboard in the darkness. And she suggested that she had the antidote to his emptiness. Had it right there, with her.

There we go, a car; a dark Audi with blacked-out windows. He thought he had seen the car stopping there before. The woman slowly straightened her cheap, light-blue handbag and jiggled her buttocks, which were squeezed into a denim skirt.

The front door of the car opened and a palm flashed in the darkness. They always stretched out a hand but never showed their faces. *He who has a cock has a business card, but they don't get them both out at the same time*, he thought, almost pitying the gipsy. She bent down and said something to the driver; she didn't seem to be in a hurry to get in. Painfully he imagined her tight skirt dropping, revealing the cherry beneath her underwear – that was what the guy in the Audi was negotiating over now. Annoyed, he tossed away the cigarette butt and closed the window.

It was nearly nine and dark but the phone was still silent. He checked the screen of his mobile – nobody had called or texted. The donuts were inedible; it was criminal selling them when they were so out of date. He threw them in the rubbish bin. But then suddenly he changed his mind and took them back out, put them into a paper bag and, still in his slippers, went down to the yard. He left the bag on the rubbish bin; it wouldn't be long before they disappeared.

'Probably you don't know . . . but maybe you do.'

The nervous voice behind him reminded him, somehow, of the hand in the Audi. He turned, startled. A woman wearing a black linen hat was standing so close to him that he could smell cheap vermouth on her breath. Her skinny body was drowned in a black garment from which protruded a pale face, distorted by sorrow. He stepped back and breathed in, ready to defend himself.

'Probably you don't know him. I'm looking for my former teacher, Kazimieras Ulbiskis. He must be very old by now, with grey . . .'

'Where does he live?'

'That's the thing, I don't know. I saw him in this yard not long ago; he was hanging around the bins – if you see what I mean?' The woman's eyes filled with tears. 'Then I, you know, I didn't have the courage to talk to him – I thought he might be embarrassed. But, you see, I came back; all the time I've been thinking about him, so maybe you know something . . .'

'I don't know, I haven't seen him,' Liudas replied impatiently. He waited for the woman to ask him for some money, but she just went on and on. Tears froze in her eyes, trembling like water in wine glasses.

'I don't know. I don't know,' he repeated, turning back towards the landing. 'Ask somebody on the ground floor.'

Back in his apartment he couldn't get the woman out of his head.

Something rustled in his son's room. He listened and was almost glad; as if his son had not left, but had just fallen asleep reading a book. Quietly, as if afraid to wake him, he opened the door to the room slightly and pressed the light switch. Startled, the furniture was woken by the light. The writing table, an empty chair on wheels he had brought from the office, shelves full of books and models, the bed covered with a knitted spread, the chest of draws for his clothes, the straw crane on the windowsill with a dried poppy seed in its beak – his son's room was the only thing that breathed any life into the apartment. He felt his heart squeeze. *What was it that I heard rustling?* he muttered. *It was probably just in my head.*

He went back into the other room which was full of books and clothes and looked out through the window – the bag of donuts was still on the rubbish bin but the woman had gone.

Just switch the TV on, he thought, *and the humming in your ears will stop.*

At that moment the ring of his mobile phone pierced the silence.

He picked up the phone and for a moment just gazed at his son's name shining on the screen and probably for the first time during his son's holiday he was reluctant to answer. Having waited all evening for the call, this hesitation confused him.

'Hi, Gailius,' he answered, at last.

'Liudas . . .' It was her. She sounded very far away; far away behind the trees and the stones and the shining road signs.

He knew immediately something had happened.

'What is it?'

Her breath came jerkily, pushing random sounds from her lungs, as always when she was searching for words.

'What has . . . Gailius . . .?'

There was a strange squeak at the other end of the line.

'Are you alone? Who is there? Isabel?' He could feel that there was somebody moving next to her.

'The ambulance is here . . . the police . . .'

'I'm coming,' he snapped, his voice dry and sharp. He disconnected the call so that he would not hear more than he could handle.

In the yard the bag with the donuts had gone.

I knew it, he thought. That could have been expected.

THE CAR slid smoothly along the sun stitched road. Looking at the trembling light and the tapestry of shadows, he felt nothing but sadness; it was the same with anything that held his gaze for more than a moment. Even the sound of a match hitting the wooden parquet floor, having over-shot the rubbish bin. The pain never left him. Occasionally, for a moment, he would forget about it, or become inured to it, like a pulsing vein in the temple, until something reminded him of it again.

Driving through the woods Liudas was stopped by a teenager, deeply suntanned, barefoot, with rolled up trousers and a dirty shirt.

'Can you drop me at the Kurpiskiai bend?' he asked through the rolled down window, his vowels dragging in the local accent.

Liudas didn't know him.

The boy settled next to him, resting a bag full of yellowing mushrooms between his knees and fixing his half open eyes on the road. He was talkative. He was from the neighbouring village and was going to Kurpiskiai to drop off the mushrooms. Liudas was suspicious that the boy was drunk, though he couldn't smell alcohol. The smell of the mushrooms was unpleasant, like damp soil.

Liudas lit a cigarette.

'Can I have one?' the boy asked casually.

Liudas thrust the packet of Wall Street cigarettes towards him.

'When did you start smoking?'

'I was born with a cigarette between my lips.' The teenager smiled like an old man; he had probably heard the phrase somewhere and decided to use it.

The boy only stopped talking when he was taking a drag on the cigarette. The shadows of alders slipped across their faces and Liudas barely listened to him, as if afraid he might hear the tap of the match on the floor.

'A child got stabbed here just recently,' the boy said, suddenly, when they had nearly reached the Kurpiskiai bend. 'The killer came right into the yard, but they couldn't catch him . . . Some kind of psychopath from prison, they reckon.'

The car swerved, momentarily, onto the opposite side of the road.

'Hey, watch out!' the boy shouted.

Liudas straightened the car.

'Let me out here.'

Liudas realised he had passed the bend. He stopped and put the car into reverse. The boy's bag smelt of sludge. The boy thanked him, slammed the door and strolled off thoughtfully along the road to Kurpiskiai.

There were only a couple of kilometres left until the turn to Puskai where the woods started. The lukewarm September sun spilled across the landscape like molten gold. Somewhere beyond the golden mist a dog howled and he knew instinctively that he was remembering it rather than hearing it.

The woods slid away from the road like a tablecloth; a clearing with a view of the farm opened up. The sunken, run down cottage had been painted green with white shutters, but now it looked washed out by the rain and time, burnt out by the sun, weathered by the wind. It looked as grey as a house martin's nest.

The yard was empty. He had heard, at the funeral, that Isabel might have sold her car.

Liudas parked his Opel next to the well, in his old spot and waited for a moment; waited for a shadow in the window, for the door to creak – for something to betray that she had heard him.

The windows were shut. There were no longer any heavy blossomed peonies under the kitchen window. The dew had taken forever to dry in their over-ripe petals that were the size of a child's palm and which would slap gently on the rain-flattened soil. The flower garden around the house was thick with weeds; daisies grew chaotically around the yard, mixed with clover in the uncut grass. From between the foundation stones shone a couple of clumps of pansies. The shadow of a hawk slid across the grass.

The pain that overwhelmed him was pitiless.

Liudas got out of the car and walked round the house. Not once did he glance at the barn, but he felt its stifling silence, as if it hadn't got its breath back after all that had happened there.

The sudden squeak of a door pierced his temples.

Again, he wasn't sure if he actually heard the sound or simply remembered it, but the door to the house really was open and swinging in the wind.

Before they had used to hold it open with a chair on which Isabel would sit and, in a few deft lines, sketch a phantasmagorical image – a wreath of people, plants or animals transfused into the same state. The lines were light and alive even when she barely touched the paper. She would draw in pencil in one of Gailius' books and leave the pictures everywhere as if to annoy Liudas, or as if she was trying to tell him something. From aside it just looked like her general absentmindedness.

Liudas never mentioned Isabel's drawings or thought about why he avoided looking at them. He would gather them up and put them in a cardboard box in the veranda and in the winter Isabel would burn them.

Liudas paused on the threshold. In the porch there was a new straw mat. The sewing table, not in use any more, had been pushed against the south wall, under the window. Thyme was drying on a heap of old newspapers. He hadn't noticed that several weeks before; he had felt, only, that something had changed, that there had been an attempt at renewal, a screening away of the exhausting past – but it had been done doubtfully and inconsistently.

He knocked on the door jamb and waited. Nothing.

Isabel was sitting at the kitchen table, her hands like empty plates on the clean oilcloth, staring in front of her. She must have seen Liudas through the window approaching along the path, but she hadn't moved.

Liudas noticed straight away that she had changed.

Her hair declared it.

She had never let it down during the day. Only at night. She would comb it for a long time at the window, trembling as the desire rose in her, as if she was excited by her own hair that spread in shiny strands over her back and shoulders.

Isabel had cut her hair.

During the funeral it had been hidden under a black, velvet scarf and Liudas couldn't understand what it was, apart from the mourning, that was different about her.

Black didn't suit Isabel. It emphasised the paleness of her skin, confined her already tiny body into an ascetic case. At the cemetery she was held up by two elderly women – one from Kurpiskiai, while the other he did not recognise. This second woman was trembling from the cold even though she was wearing a coat with a sheepskin collar at the end of August. The trembling, though it mirrored Isabel's, was not from mourning and that, for some reason, annoyed Liudas.

At the funeral Beatrice went over to greet Isabel. She kissed her shyly at the temple, stopping near the skin as if she wasn't sure she was allowed that level of intimacy.

Eimuntas Brasiskis, who was a well-known and valued architect in some circles, was standing some way off, under the trees, keeping his eye on his wife, Beatrice. Liudas' glance swept over Brasiskis' round face. Brasiskis nodded and then hastily fixed his eyes back on Beatrice, as if afraid he might have missed something.

When Liudas took over from the woman and held Isabel by the elbow, she moved slightly, as if turning over in her sleep and looked right through him, as if she didn't recognise him. They talked – or rather exchanged an insignificant phrase or two – communicating as if through rippling water. It was the others that caused the ripples. They were gathered in a black ring around the hole, their hands folded piously. They kept asking Liudas about things he didn't understand, about topics too far removed from that hole with the rustling conifer wreaths. The whispered questions jarred against the solemnly clasped hands. Life throbbed in them.

They did not look at each other. Liudas held her sharp, cold elbow like it was an umbrella handle and he was waiting for its owner to turn up and free him from the encumbrance of it. The fact was, Isabel's despair was too heavy for him; he couldn't cope with it. Right from birth he had avoided having to deal with difficult things. He attempted to keep his thoughts quick and simple. And today perhaps faster than usual, so his thoughts wouldn't linger or explode into a painful fear and the ghost of self-pity.

While Brasiskis had disappeared somewhere, Beatrice sparkled still among the procession of mourners. Though she kept herself at a distance, her facial expressions communicated themselves clearly, much to Liudas' irritation. He didn't, however, have the patience to try and interpret the signs she sent him. Liudas had found it easy to get used to not thinking about her during the few years they had not seen each other. After the ceremony Beatrice's thick perfume enveloped him and he realised he was standing next to her lithe body. She was dressed in an expensive black suit; he looked at her carelessly and with half closed eyes, as if at an old black and white photograph, trying to remember what they used to have in common.

Beatrice was still beautiful. She was packaged in such a civilised way, with her black curls glistening like coal in the sunlight. When Beatrice moved there spread around her waves of blood, and black soil, and of gold and almonds. She had the sharpness of petals and the dew-freshness of bubbles in a wineglass. It wasn't important whether it was her hair, the twitch of her wrist or of her hip, each moved in the same scented manner. But it was all too subtle for Liudas. The remnants of any feelings he might have had could not be revived by that faint sensation of déjà vu.

'She needs to be looked after,' Beatrice said, watching as Isabel was led to the car.

Liudas didn't reply. He stared, as if hypnotized, at the back of Isabel's white neck below her black beret. Her relatives behaved as if she were a fragile piece of furniture that might break at any moment.

They ignored Liudas. He thought that, beneath their politeness, they were cold to him and, without noticing it, he withdrew. He would have liked to have held Isabel's hand, just to have held her fingers companionably in his own, but he couldn't imagine how he could have done this in the presence of her relatives. It was as if he had betrayed their property and now he had no right to touch it. The bunch of them in their black clothes had made it clear that Liudas could stand next to his son's body only because they allowed him to do so. And that was their first, last and only concession to a man who had left a woman with an epileptic son.

How terrible, dear, how terrible . . . if the poor woman hadn't been left on her own in some forgotten corner this might not have happened. Liudas could hear how the women in hats whispered.

'You know, it's a strange coincidence but . . . Ilya disappeared that night,' Beatrice whispered.

'What are you talking about?'

'I'm just telling you . . .'

'Beatrice, our game was over a long time ago.'

'I know. You still think I'm interested? Hilarious.'

'What do you want?'

'Nothing. I won't let anybody else know that he disappeared, because if I did we would have to divulge our little story as well; all the misunderstandings over the adoption and so on. I don't want to lose my job. Do you understand?'

'If you don't want to say anything about it, that's fine. You can start by not saying anything now.' Liudas was annoyed.

Hurt, Beatrice turned and disappeared among the conifers and grave stones, leaving the scent of her perfume in his nose.

But her words wouldn't leave him. From that moment Beatrice's careless revelation at the cemetery began to obsess Liudas, even in his sleep.

His apartment was unbearably stuffy. When he got back from the funeral he sat gazing at the Venetian mask as if seeing it for the first time. The mask stared back, pulling faces at something behind him. But the moment he turned to see what had caused the mask's sour expression, it, whatever it was, turned too, staying behind him. The mask chuckled spitefully.

Suddenly glittery tears began to pour from its slanted eyeholes. Liudas flinched and it was a moment before he realised it was he who was crying and not the mask.

He stood in the doorway, examining Isabel's bloodless profile, the small, upward tilt to her nose and her regular, beautiful chin with a black mole which looked like a bread crumb dropped in milk. He decided to wait until she turned round so that he didn't scare her. But Isabel didn't move; under half lowered eye lids her irises looked as if they were covered in dust – she didn't blink nor did she see anything. The only thing that gave any hint that she was alive was the slightly visible pulsing above her collarbone where the dress ended.

Liudas lit a cigarette, opened the kitchen window and blew out the smoke. Immediately he felt uneasy because of the noise he had caused. It was a brutal invasion of Isabel's silence, but he couldn't turn back. The sound awoke Isabel and she moved, inhaled and blinked.

'The grass needs cutting,' Liudas said looking out through the window.

'I'll do it,' she replied.

Isabel's voice was calm, but there was something different in its tone. Liudas flicked the ash through the window and, sensing Isabel's gaze, turned round quickly.

'So how are you?' Liudas asked, annoyed that his voice trembled.

'Fine.'

'Does anybody visit you?'

She was silent. The silence was like the shell of an egg; if it was broken she would die like a premature chick, but Liudas couldn't stop himself.

'What?' she asked, her eyes still lowered, her voice a pulse beneath her neck.

'How are you doing here, on your own?'

'I'm fine.'

He put out the cigarette in the bowl of soapy water and stuck his head into porch, then turned round.

'Where's the scythe?

'Don't touch it. I'll do it.'

'Make me some coffee, I'll just . . .'

'Don't touch anything, do you understood?' Though she

didn't raise her voice, it was an unequivocal edict. Liudas' enthusiasm was dampened immediately; he sat down on the out-of-use tiled stove and, to give himself something to do with his hands, lit another cigarette.

Isabel moved again. Remembering suddenly that she was the hostess, she gathered up all of her strength and rose from the table. Liudas watched with growing horror as she sluggishly brought three cups from the stove to the table, one by one, moving as if through sticky resin. She lined them up in an insanely accurate line and leisurely cleaned them with her apron.

Her features had faded. In place of her face there was left only a naked, half-dead surface, like a mirror obscured by dust, standing in front of which you could see no reflection.

'It was you who told me to leave. If you hadn't . . .'

'Don't.'

'If I had been with you . . .'

Isabel inspected the cups. Then she took them back to the stove, one by one. The way she moved was horrible; it was as if she were trapped inside a tight coffin. There was no openness in her movements; the old, graceful Isabel who had trembled in the slightest breeze was gone, leaving only hard granite and death. Liudas closed his eyes and shrank away from her. Ignoring him, Isabel settled back at the table and lowered her gaze to somewhere between her palms, as if they were somehow useless now.

'What happened here? Who was here?' Liudas asked, pulling himself together.

She didn't reply.

'Did you see him?'

'Who?' Her lips barely moved. She didn't turn, though she seemed to have expected the question.

'Who did it?'

Being behind her, he saw how Isabel's shoulders tensed.

'Beatrice said that Ilya ran away that night.'

'Do you live with her?'

'No. Isabel . . .'

'Why?'

Was she worried only about that? 'Was it Ilya?'

She was silent.

'It was Ilya, Isabel, wasn't it? What did you say to police? You saw him, didn't you? Why don't you say so?'

'No.'

'What, "no"?'

'I didn't see him,' she said then, coldly. And that was it.

They sat together for a long time, not looking at each other; it was as if they were unable to break their pointless, depressing dependence on each other. It was as if they were waiting for something, but dared not confess it. Liudas gave in first.

'I'll stay.'

'Go, Liudas. Go. Leave,' Isabel repeated in an indifferent tone. It was as if she were referring to the life of some other woman. Only a tearful impatience sharpened her words.

Liudas put his head in his hands and swayed gently as if he was trying to calm himself, or to lull himself like an idiot. Nothing helped. He grabbed a cup from the stove, one of those Isabel had just placed with the others and threw it on the floor.

The cup didn't shatter. Only the handle bluntly clattered as it fell off and slipped down between the floorboards.

'Come with me,' Liudas said as calmly as he could.

'No.'

'You can't stay here on your own. I'll bring you back when you want me to.'

'Leave me. Please. Leave,' Isabel whispered.

Losing his patience, Liudas went out to the yard. It was quiet and calm and hushed. The soft fleece of the woods seemed to be waiting to see what Liudas would do next. The woods belonged to Isabel. Liudas lit a cigarette and circled the car looking for a place to stand. He threw down the cigarette and ran back into the kitchen. Isabel hadn't moved.

'Can I at least visit you from time to time?' he asked nervously.

'It's you who are afraid of being on your own.'

'Just to check how you're doing?'

It seemed to Liudas that the corner of Isabel's lip turned up in a smile.

'To talk, well . . .'

'What do we have to talk about, Liudas?' For the first time she lifted her eyes to him. It so frightened him that he stepped backwards and collided with the doorframe. That hadn't happened for many years. Recovering himself, he put his hand to his throat and mumbled, 'I'll come again.'

That night Liudas had a lot to drink. He called some women and then went to a bar to meet somebody and, having drunk himself half to death, had a fight with a bouncer.

The next morning he had some more to drink and then crushed the Venetian mask. It had no right to hang on his wall and smirk as if it had seen more than him. Nobody had the right to look at Liudas and ask him how he was doing.

You had to ask before you could look into somebody's eyes.

He didn't set foot in the boy's room.

At the office he told the girls he was going away for a couple of weeks.

A FOX used to come onto the orphanage grounds. It didn't come through the hole in the lattice fence but through the gate like everybody else. Its fur, which was the colour of mountain ash, would flash among the tree trunks like a brush dipped in paint. At first they were afraid the fox might be rabid and forbade the children from approaching it. The guard set traps. But the fox began coming every day, avoiding the traps and it soon became clear that, despite the prohibition, the older children were taming it. When she found out about this, Beatrice allowed them to feed the fox with the leftovers from the kitchen.

Not long after, the fox disappeared. The smaller children were upset; they had been taking out treats for the fox and leaving them at the gates – if it was in a good mood, it would stick its nose out of the nut wood and wait until they were gone.

About a week later the guard found it near the road. The fox's fur no longer flamed, it lay in a heap in the moss, like a small mound of leaves. The guard kicked it and turned it over. The light fur on its chest was sticky with blood, at its throat there was a black wound. He hid the carcass in the undergrowth; in the evening he went back with a spade and buried it.

They told the children the fox had had babies and would not come back any more. When they have a litter, they explained, they have to forget about fun and games and look after their little ones. Animals often understand that better than people, they told the children.

Ilya, however, already knew that all fairy-tale beginnings ended sooner or later when reality set in. Every day they took something from you; if you were given a present it was only so they could take it away again. *The Evil One* who played cruelly with you, did so for *his* own pleasure, Ilya felt; he knew that *he* existed. *He* throbbed on the outskirts of Ilya's imagination. Sometimes *he* crept into his dreams, but he could never picture *him*. *He* would spill like ink behind Ilya and breathe on the back of his neck – the icy breath would make his hair stand on end.

Ilya was not afraid of *him*. He hated *him*.

When he was sent back to the orphanage from Puskai, he would hit anybody who dared to approach him or look him in the eyes. Nobody had the right to ask him any questions.

He swapped some chewing gum with one of the boys for a knife.

The fox didn't manage to bear its litter.

He hid the knife, wrapped in a cellophane film, in the park next to the lattice fence. He had thought of this himself; secrets should be kept in the ground. They needed to be saved for rainy days and then taken out at the right time. Nobody knew when they would be needed or for whom, but they were necessary.

Another thing he knew was that secrets were a terrible thing.

Four years later everybody had forgotten about the fox. A young deer came to the woods behind the orphanage fence. She was trusting and, so long as they didn't get too close, would let the children watch her. Seeing her took Ilya's breath away. She had wide eyes and her fur was patterned beautifully with small leaf-like shapes, her slim legs were graceful and would quiver with a wild, impatient, mercurial force. The slightest unexpected sound disturbed the deer. She would tilt her elegant neck and then she was gone; leaving nothing more than a faint stirring among the branches of the trees.

She was so quiet and sad and so incredibly pretty it touched Ilya's heart, so that involuntarily he squeezed his fist as if clenching a knife. He stood at the fence and waited for the deer to appear among the glistening leaves of the lime trees and gazed into her melancholy eyes. He knew at what times she would appear, as if they had agreed upon them. But he would grow weak as he stood waiting, and when he saw her his heart would contract so painfully that it was clear it had to end.

He could not afford to be weak.

One day Ilya dug up the knife and left the orphanage. He returned the next morning delirious and with empty hands from which he tried to rinse a frightening feeling of stickiness. The river water couldn't wash it away, even though he scrubbed his hands thoroughly, even under the nails.

Ilya never touched the knife again. Neither the one at the bottom of the river nor any other.

When, a couple of days later, the deer poked her nose among the leaves of the lime tree, Ilya cried – at first silently and then, later, painfully, louder. But only for her. The deer was not surprised; it sniffed at the air sympathetically, as if it wished to taste the boy's tears.

From that night on Ilya waited for them to come for him.

LIUDAS ARRIVED in the afternoon when the smaller children were having a nap. The older children went out to play, away from the buildings, so as not to wake up the sleeping ones. The nurses would leave them on their own and while the girls would scatter around the park the boys would kick the ball around in the stadium.

Ilya was not the type to hang around with the others. He had his friends and with them he would slip, unobserved, out of the orphanage territory into the woods; sometimes he even went as far as the river beyond the road. Most often he went alone.

Liudas left his car in the woods and strolled to the orphanage on foot. In the yard a group of fifteen children were kicking up a racket. Two elderly nurses shouted at them to line up in twos. Liudas stopped by the fence, hidden by the rosehip bush and pulled out a pair of binoculars.

The children were about to go on an outing. In the summer they would take the children to a small creek. Sand would be dumped there in the summer to make a beach and lemon-yellow buoys marked the area where they were allowed to swim. That day it was too cool for swimming, but on a sunny September morning it was a nice place for an outing, with rugs, balls and badminton racquets. 'E-ve-li-ne, where's your cap?' shouted the plump head nurse. 'Modestas! Mo-des-tas, I'm speaking to you. I won't say it again! Ilya, Ilya! You're the last one; we're waiting for you!'

Liudas listened, searching with his binoculars until he caught site of the sullen face with the dark almond eyes. Ilya kept a distance from others. He was flicking stones with a stick and seemed hesitant. Liudas recognised immediately the expression which would invariably distort Ilya's face when he was about to get into trouble.

Before the children reached the gate Liudas rushed back through the woods to the car.

Liudas was first to reach the creek. He hid the car further away, on a track with low bushes obscuring it, then settled himself on a cliff overgrown with pine trees. From there the beach could be seen clearly.

The procession appeared after a good half hour. Their colourful coats flashed between the pine trunks, disappeared and then reappeared again at the bottom of the cliff close to the water. Liudas lifted the binoculars to his eyes.

He could see that Ilya was up to something and was looking for the opportunity to get away from the crowd. At one end of the beach the girls put down some rugs and placed on them the bags with food and their coats. The nurses organised a ball game. The red head clapped her hands to get their attention and urged the children to come closer.

It was then that Ilya dived into the bulrushes.

Liudas ran, following him along the cliff, crossing the path to the beach along which the children had just descended. Soon the cover of bushes along the bank was gone; the water glittered down below and Liudas again saw the runner moving quickly. Without thinking he jumped and slid down the cliff.

Ilya stopped and turned, startled.

Liudas grabbed him by his elbow, locked it in his grip. And that gave him away.

'Hi, Illya,' Liudas said, out of breath.

'Uh, hi . . .'

'How are you?'

'Fine.'

'Listen, we need to talk.'

Without explaining further, he dragged the child along the bank to where the brushwood began, where there were thick bulrushes growing in the water. They dove into the thick of the woods like birds looking for a place for a nest. Liudas did not let go of the child for a second. His face hovered over Ilya's as if over a crystal ball – as if searching for an answer in his face before even asking a question.

Ilya lifted his eyes to Liudas and blinked; the silver grains glistened in his irises.

'I know you ran away one night, recently.' Liudas spoke slowly and clearly, keeping his sharp gaze on Ilya. Ilya did not move. His eyes were black and opaque, like packed earth.

'Is it true?' Liudas said. 'Don't deny it, I know.'

'So why are you asking?' Ilya snapped. He grinned with the false sincerity of an experienced orphan.

Liudas, struggling to hold himself back, squeezed the child's pointed chin.

'Don't give me those innocent eyes . . . tell me where you were that night,' he hissed.

'Nowhere,' Ilya answered calmly. 'I was asleep.'

It was possible that there were secrets, treasures, nightmares hidden in the black soil of his eyes, but Liudas had no idea how to dig them out. He squeezed Ilya's cheekbones harder, as if threatening to force out the right answer.

'You're a lying, little animal . . . There's no way you were sleeping.'

'Ask the headmistress if you don't believe me,' Ilya shot back.

Suddenly Liudas understood.

Understood who was behind him, who encouraged his arrogance.

Liudas squeezed the child's face with both palms and shook it with contempt, as if he were trying to crush it.

'If I found out that you ran away – I would grind you into dust. Understood? Do you understand?'

He let him go suddenly and Ilya stepped back almost losing his balance.

'Get back to the rest. Quickly!'

The black soil in Ilya's irises smouldered; his contempt mirrored that in Liudas' distorted face. For a couple of seconds their gazes clashed, as if they were testing who was stronger. Ilya gave in first – or perhaps postponed the fight for a better time. He turned his back on Liudas and, with his hands stuck in his pockets, strolled hastily through the tall grass back to the children.

Returning to the car, Liudas headed straight to Puskai.

Wind ruffled the high grass in the yard. A bowl filled with soapy water and several dirty plates stood near the well. A flock of starlings exploded from the grass and flew towards the woods.

The door was locked from the inside. Liudas knocked at each of the windows, but nothing happened. He couldn't get rid of the feeling that Isabel was inside.

'Isabel, open up, or I'll break the door!' Liudas shouted, losing his patience.

There was no response. The grass blew in the wind and then was still. Once again Liudas walked round the house, going up into the veranda beneath the apple tree. In the veranda, next to an empty three litre jar, stood a canister of petrol. Without thinking, Liudas leant forward and glued his face to the glass door. Isabel's face, pale and flat with large, feverish eyes, swam into focus in the window looking out onto the garden. Her eyes dominated her other features; even her small body sagged under the wrinkles of her dress – as if the fire in her eyes had consumed Isabel from the inside. Liudas opened his mouth to say something, but Isabel put a finger to her lips and shook her head conspiratorially. He gestured for her to open the window. She opened it a fraction.

'Wrong time. Come another day,' she whispered.

'When, Isabel?'

'I'll call you.'

'Call tomorrow.'

'I will call.'

'In the morning, Isabel.'

'Fine.'

'Or I'll call you tomorrow.'

'Fine, okay.'

Carefully, quietly she closed the window, drew the net curtains, and with her finger still against her lips, walked backwards until she disappeared into the dusk of the room.

Liudas felt a knot in his throat. At first the thought struck him that he should go to town for help. Standing next to his car, he gazed for a long time at the empty windows of the house, behind which Isabel flamed. He couldn't make up his mind what to do. It was getting dark and he didn't dare leave Isabel alone. He couldn't imagine who he could bring without scaring her. Who he could entrust her to.

He steered out of the yard, hid his car in the thick of the woods and checked if the sleeping bag was still in the boot. From the ferns, fifty metres from the car, he could see the house and the yard up to the barn. The door, it was true, was on the other side of the house, towards the fields, but there was no place to hide there.

He sprayed himself with anti-mosquito liquid, placed the sleeping bag on the groundsheet in the ferns, in the woods, his binoculars strung around his neck.

It was calm for a couple of hours. At dusk the tune on his mobile phone suddenly played. Liudas hissed and hastily pressed the button. It was Beatrice.

'Hi,' she said. Her voice suggested nothing good.

'Good evening.'

'Where are you?'

'Why are you bothered?

'I wondered if you were still standing guard on the orphanage.'

Liudas was silent.

'They saw your car outside our building today.'

'Really? They might have been mistaken.'

'What are you up to, Liudas?'

'What do you want, Beatrice?'

'Are you trying to catch Ilya? Don't you understand – you won't catch him. He didn't do anything, I talked to him. That night he was with another group, more of the hopeless cases. They get cigarettes from somewhere and play cards for them. He never left, do you understand?'

'You got confused yourself.'

'I won't testify otherwise, if necessary.'

They were quiet. He couldn't hear her breathing, only a stiff silence on her end of the line.

'Leave Ilya alone. Do you hear?'

'Bye, Beatrice!' Liudas cut off the connection and switched the phone to silent, so that he could still check the time on its screen.

The wind died down towards the evening, only the birds trilled gently. The house sank into the dusk. The three windows of the large room which were visible to Liudas from the ferns were dark – Isabel was probably in the kitchen, as she had been on his last visit, or perhaps in the smaller room. Or perhaps she had self-combusted from the fire in her deranged eyes.

It grew cooler. Liudas fetched a jumper and a coat from the car. He smoked, shielding the tip of the cigarette in case Isabel glanced through the window.

Somehow he fell asleep. It seemed as though he had slept for only a moment.

He was woken by the sound of crackling and a restless light on the other side of his eye lids.

A strong smell of disaster filled his lungs – he jumped up, his eyes not yet fully open, disorientated.

The end of the yard was shining. The crown of the fire reached up into the sky.

Only then did it occur to him; the barn was burning. In the firelight the reddish bones of the planks crackled and roared. They broke loudly, eaten away by the fire.

The sparks, lifted by the hot air, rose into the black sky, then descended further way, on the grass,

on Isabel.

Liudas did not notice her until he was in the yard.

Isabel stood on the path, leaning forwards, her arms pressed to her sides. She wore a light cotton dress with a tiny flower-pattern that shone white in the darkness, like a veil. Beneath her short cropped hair the bones of her spine protruded like rosary beads. She stood too close to the fire, as if she had been created of the very same substance. With her eyes wide open, she stared at the flames' wild tongues. She didn't hear Liudas. Only when he grabbed her by the hand and pulled her away from the fire, did she jump, staring at him with empty eyes.

Isabel scrutinized Liudas from deep within her feverish eyes. Curiously, leisurely, she shifted her attention from the fire to him. It was as if she were looking at him for the first time, like the fire. A ghastly, deranged interest.

Suddenly Liudas remembered the petrol canister in the veranda.

Isabel's pupils widened, her face wrinkled like smouldering paper and she began to cry. 'Mama.' Her mouth moved without making a sound. 'Ma-ma.' She trembled. She looked at Liudas, begging him to cover her eyes, to cover her and help her sleep.

Some people appeared from the side of the field, behind the alder trees, their clothes pale against the darkness.

Furiously, Liudas pulled Isabel to himself and pressed her hot face against his chest, probably too hard – he could feel her nose pressed through his jumper, but Isabel didn't resist.

Fortunately, there was no wind.

There were people approaching. Liudas recognised Juozas Garnys and Pranciska; behind them another couple of people from Kurpiskiai were rushing towards them. They jumped from the darkness into the yard, golden from the fire, their faces orange, their eyes glowing beneath furrowed foreheads. Liudas waved to them.

His other hand still pressed Isabel to his chest to prevent her from seeing and thinking; then there would be no fear, no heartache, no questions – just the pure, wound-cleansing flame. Liudas would do anything for her. Liudas would be the cover Isabel longed for, under which she could hide safely from her troubles.

He listened to Isabel's breathing grow calmer.

She did not resist.

*   *   *

WHEN SHE entered Liudas' flat, Isabel went straight to the window. On the opposite bank of the river, the windows in the skyscraper sparkled like sharpened knives.

Liudas pointed to the windows of his travel agency and she nodded. The play of the sunlight was different in the city to how it had been in the woods; the large, sharp shadows that fell from the buildings looked like still pools of tar. The occasional tree shed a rounded, familiar shadow onto the asphalt. It was true there was a river in the city too, wide and fast and unsuitable for swimming, but you could go down the steps to it and sit on the concrete paving and dangle your feet into the water.

Liudas suggested that Isabel did just that, but it took her a couple of weeks to pluck up the courage. So far she had only asked for some water. She drank it all.

While Liudas was pulling Isabel's rucksack from the car, her eyes half closed and her features sharpened – as they did when something drew her interest. Instinctively, he looked in the direction in which her gaze fell – a grey, bearded man was digging through the rubbish bin, his head in the container.

'Let's go,' Liudas said.

Later he could not pull Isabel from the window. She was not hungry; she drank some mineral water thirstily and then quietly placed the glass next to the sink.

'So this is where you live,' she said, absentmindedly, having looked round the living room.

Suddenly her eye caught the glass door. She moved towards it, but Liudas, having expected this, stood in the way.

'No, not in there, Isabel.'

Gently, as if apologetically, he took her elbow – Isabel's skin was cool and waxy, as if it had been polished – and turned her towards the small room with the arch.

After the funeral Liudas had scrubbed the floor and placed the books in the corner and covered them with an old sheet. He had also pushed in there the artificial leather sofa he had used to sleep on in the living room and a three legged coffee table from the room with the glass door.

'Here.' Liudas led Isabel through the arch and gently propelled her towards the sofa where her rucksack was – a sign that it would be her space. Obediently she sat down; her leg fell into a patch of sunlight that trembled on her sun tanned foot which was as narrow as the petal of a clematis. On her ankle was a black spot from a mosquito bite. Liudas' heart lurched; he looked round trying to remember where he had placed the woman's slippers he had bought.

'Is this your room?' she asked, when she had put the slippers on.

'This is your room,' Liudas answered.

While he was making coffee, Isabel slumbered on the sofa. Liudas jumped when she appeared behind him and asked where the bathroom was. He accompanied her. He heard the lock click. The flush followed but Isabel didn't come out. Ten minutes later Liudas quietly knocked on the door.

'Isabel . . . Is-a-bel . . .'

'Eh –' she called.

'What are you doing in there?'

'Nothing.'

'Can I come in?'

'I can't unlock the door . . . I can't do it,' she said.

Liudas pushed the door and it opened – she hadn't even locked it properly. She was sat on the edge of the bath looking hazy; the straps of her dress had fallen off her shoulders, the pink, fake-fur slippers were under the bath.

Liudas showed her how to use the lock.

'There's no need to lock it,' he added.

Isabel didn't seem to hear.

At dusk it grew gloomy. The shadows got longer; they distorted and spilled across the apartment as if they were ink. The street lights didn't come on for a long time and Liudas had to switch on the lamp above the cooker. The meagre light it threw from the corner of the kitchen wasn't enough to illuminate the spacious living room and the far end drowned in the darkness.

The gipsy was not around and Liudas, watching the orange tip of his cigarette as it fell towards the street, was flooded once more with pain.

In Isabel's room he heard the rucksack being unzipped, the crackle of a plastic bag and then all went quiet again. Soon, from the darkness came a soft yawning, sounding like a squashed gasp.

'Switch on the light,' Liudas called.

Without leaving the cooker, he explained where the switch was.

An amber light licked across the floor through the arch.

Liudas took a clean set of bed linen and made Isabel's bed. Had she brought her nightie? Isabel became thoughtful as if he had posed an impossibly complex question. She seemed alarmed that she had to do something with all these foreign objects – to switch them on, to lift them up, to put them on, to open, to push to another place. Her eyes shuttled back and forth, feverishly looking for an escape, hoping to avoid the activities, to hide between the gaps of the parquet, to fuse with the dust raised by the blankets.

Liudas put a shirt on the pillow.

Isabel changed with the lights off as there was no door to her room.

In the living room Liudas turned to the window – the gipsy still hadn't arrived and he was suddenly worried something might have happened to her.

Then he heard the sheets rustle. He put the TV on with the volume low and asked Isabel if she wanted to watch a film. She didn't. Was the sound too loud? No. As the sofa had been pushed into Isabel's room for her bed, he settled on the floor in front of the screen. The chair, in the lamp-lit corner, seemed too far away; it was out of reach.

When the film ended, Liudas, on his way to the bathroom, could see Isabel lying on her bed with her eyes wide open, arms stretched out over the covers, lit by the blue street light. He stopped in the arch.

'Don't come close to me.' Isabel's lips barely moved.

Liudas waited for a long time for her to fall asleep. At two in the morning her eyelids finally closed, and from the archway he could hear her breathing, slow and deep.

Liudas went into his son's room. It was the first time he had opened the door since his son had left.

He had been dreading that moment, but he barely felt anything at all. Nothing particularly sharp. Only the familiar scent in his nostrils. Liudas sat on the chair at the door and began to cry quietly.

How strange that things don't disappear with their owners, Liudas thought gazing at the child's pencil holder he had made out of twigs. An object is more durable than a person. A person creates something in order to somehow prolong himself and then he dies. How unfair.

Later he brushed various small things from the desk; some toys, some drawings and then some books from the shelf and put everything into a strong, blue rubbish bag and hid it in the bed linen box under the bed. The bag rustled as if unhappy at being used for that purpose. Anxiously, Liudas told it to quieten down. Often he froze and listened for any sound from behind the wall. He threw the rubber slippers and a striped jumper left on the chair into the wardrobe and hastily closed the door to stop the wave of familiar scent rising from there. He took a framed family photo from the wall and placed it in the desk drawer. On the desk, on top of a pile of exercise books, was one with pictures of wild animals on the cover. A rectangular piece of white paper was glued to its cover. 'Tragi-comical reflections on daily life,' was scribbled on the label in a child's hand. Without much thought, Liudas put it under his arm.

The room seemed to have withdrawn into itself. He ran a wet sponge over the furniture and the empty surfaces shone. They were cold and soulless; they belonged to nobody, as they had been when, with his son, he had chosen them at the shop.

Liudas switched off the light and closed the door.

Behind the wall, in the blue street light, Isabel was breathing softly.

In the morning, having showed Isabel where the most important things were, Liudas left for the travel agency. When he lifted his head from the computer he could see a small dot in his living room window across the river – Isabel would approach the window and suddenly retreat back into the depths of the room, as if she were accustomising herself to the day light.

'Did you see me waving to you?' Liudas asked at lunch time, having brought her some soup and a chicken roll from the café.

'No I didn't,' Isabel said.

She didn't touch the food he brought. She ate a bit of cheese from the fridge and took a sip of coffee.

When Liudas came back from the office in the evening, he noticed immediately that the glass door was open slightly. Isabel was lying on the child's bed, curled up like a caterpillar, Gailius' shirt pressed to her chest. Her knuckles were white, as if the bones had rubbed through the skin.

'Isabel,' he whispered.

'Get out.'

But the next day she waved to Liudas from the window. She raised her hand clumsily, as if it were too heavy, like a station officer instructing a train to pass. Between them the river sparkled painfully. For some reason Liudas worried Isabel wouldn't be able to lower her arm and he sighed with relief when her hand slid down towards her side and hid itself among the folds of her clothes. She was wearing something brightly patterned and Liudas, coming home for lunch, recognised his old shirt with red and purple diamonds.

The smell of cleaning fluid filled the living room.

'You cleaned the floor?' Liudas was surprised.

'Don't give me away to anybody,' Isabel said, suddenly, looking straight into his eyes.

She sat at the table with her bare legs folded under her, the bright diamonds of the shirt reflecting in her hollow cheeks.

The previous evening her cousin had called. For a quarter of an hour Liudas had to reassure her that he would be able to deal with Isabel himself. In the end, ignoring Liudas' arguments, she mentioned that she knew a doctor at the psychiatric hospital. She paused then and stopped. Annoyed, he listened for a couple of seconds to the silence, making no attempt to make it easier for her. Then he said good bye and put down the phone.

The silence in Isabel's room buzzed.

'I won't give you away,' Liudas said carelessly. 'Would you like an orange?'

Isabel glanced at the orange. She played with it in her hand, as if unsure what to do with it, but did not put it down. For the whole evening she did not let go of it; it was only later, when she dropped off watching a film, that the orange slid out of her hand and bumped against Liudas' thigh. It was warm from Isabel's hand and scented. Liudas put the orange aside, but Isabel moved and opened her eyes.

'Where's the orange?' she asked.

Liudas placed the orange back in her hand.

One Saturday morning Liudas asked, 'Would you like to go for a walk?'

Isabel shook her head. But after dinner Liudas took her chamois jacket off the hook, brought her shoes and said he would wait in the car.

They drove slowly through sun-lit fields. Imperceptibly, above them, an autumnal heaviness gathered like invisible tears. The trees knitted themselves into a dense necklace on either side of the road. The tops of the trees flashed bloodily. Light seeped through the baroque ornamentation of cloud. Above the miserable plains clusters of the cloud hovered like the broken sculptures of enormous angels – slivers of marble with light blue seams gleamed in the September sun.

Gazing out through the open sun roof of the car, Isabel described the scene so quietly that Liudas had to slow down in order to be able to hear her.

Finally she asked him to stop.

The clouds stirred. It was so calm you could almost hear how the wind polished them, how they rolled across the sky their shapes shifting slightly, how they passed each other, seeped through each other and parted, leaving a feathery trail behind them. Without a word Isabel got out of the car and walked into the tall grass.

For some time she stood there, frozen.

'Isabel,' Liudas shouted, stubbing out his cigarette.

She didn't seem to hear him. Slamming the door he walked across to Isabel. She covered her face and turned away, as always when she didn't want Liudas to see her tears. He took her by her shoulders and shook her as if to wake her up, and the eyes that she turned on him were brimming with questions. At first they were cold and foreign, but then they began to brighten.

'Let's go home,' she whispered.

On the way back they didn't speak. Mesmerised, Isabel observed how the road unfolded like a dirty bandage beneath the car. When they got back into town she could barely hold back her smile; its reflection spilled out like silk waving in the wind.

In the yard Isabel ran round the car, laughing. A couple, who were passing the gate, looked at her bemused. Liudas recognised the old man with the grey-beard. He was wearing a dark green raincoat and a strip of hair, clean and neatly combed, ran like white putty beneath his knitted beret. Holding his arm was the woman in the black coat. Liudas recognised her.

'Good evening!' he shouted.

The woman shrugged and waved. They strode on with even, tiny steps, their heads turned in one direction, as if they were sewn to each other. A sour breeze blew through the gate way.

That night Liudas couldn't hold back.

'Isabel . . . do you really not remember anything strange? You didn't see any stranger near the house?'

Isabel thought.

'No. Gailius had run out of ink and he was determined to go to Kurpiskiai. He wouldn't listen, he didn't care that it was too late and that Pranciska had probably closed the shop . . . You know what he was like. I had felt . . . I always felt that our life was a long preparation for what happened . . . such a long farewell before that . . .'

'That day – did anybody come to the house?'

'No . . . I don't remember.'

'Beatrice said . . .'

'It was not Ilya.'

'How do you know, Isabel?'

Their eyes met.

'We made a mistake taking that child on.'

'I don't regret anything,' Isabel replied coldly.

They didn't say any more about it.

On Monday evening Isabel suggested they go to the cinema.

'I want to watch a love story, something funny,' she said.

Liudas chose an American comedy.

They sat in the small, hot hall, sunk deeply in the soft, red chairs and watched the audience come in. Music played softly from the loudspeakers. Most of the people arrived in twos and joked, quietly looking for the seats marked on their tickets. Liudas noted that they all looked similar somehow.

'Maybe they're all in a similar mood,' Isabel suggested.

She sat with her jacket unbuttoned. The curls that were re-growing at her temples were damp and beads of perspiration gathered above her lip. Liudas brushed them away with his thumb.

'Take your coat off.'

Obediently, as if she had just woken up, Isabel took her jacket off and placed it on her knees.

Every single face interested her. She soaked up the expressions, the movements, the modulations of voice. Her face held the expression of an observer. She was hypnotized by the speed with which hands unwrapped a chocolate and by the way women adjusted their hair or pulled off scarves from their necks. It was like Isabel had been locked up for an eternity and was captivated, now, with faces and the cosy din of people relaxed after the working day.

The cinema was only half full when the film started. When the lights went down, Isabel let out a long sigh and then laughed at herself. They smiled at each other as if they were engaged in a secret game.

'What a joy it is to sit in soft chairs and observe huge people, whose faces fill the screen, even if they aren't very clever, or interesting and we've seen their story lots of times before,' Isabel said after the film.

The rain had just stopped. They stood under a lamp post unsure what to do next, people flooding past them.

'I want some ice cream,' Isabel said and they went to look for a shop that might still be open.

'I want to run!' she shouted and began to run as fast as she could.

Her figure, as she receded into the distance, looked as frail as beads on a thin thread. Liudas felt a knot in his throat. He quickened his pace and waved; Isabel was waiting at the crossing. Her cheeks were burning. Her tousled hair gleamed like fire in the orange street light. Unexpectedly they took each other's hands. Isabel's damp, trusting palm responded to the slightest pressure of his.

'Liudas, am I healthy now?' she asked, suddenly very serious.

'You're getting better. You're getting better very quickly,' he said.

At home, Liudas watched, mesmerised, as Isabel made sandwiches under the dim light which shone from above the cooker. Her hair had grown down to the mole on the back of her neck; the mole that he had touched for the first time twelve years before when kissing Isabel under the horse chestnut opposite the student hostel. She had been shy and asked him to remove his hand from her neck and then joked that if you pressed the button under her hair, the door to her heart would open. That night Liudas had parted her curls and kissed the magic lock to her heart – not realising he had already been granted entrance.

Liudas went across to Isabel, who was bent over the cutting board and touched the mole with his lips.

He felt a warm wave of her long forgotten scent. Breathing heavily, he kissed her back under the cotton shirt, her fragrant buttocks, the islands of skin between her shirt and jeans, covered with light, golden hairs. When Isabel turned, confused, he pressed her to his chest so hard that she grew scared and began to squirm.

'What are you doing?' she whispered, her eyes wide open.

Liudas realised nothing would come of it.

Her body didn't respond. It stood before him so painfully beautiful, but foreign. Isabel had changed the lock it seemed. The old key wouldn't open her heart.

'Will you ever forgive me that I left you both?' Liudas whispered.

'I forgave you a long time ago. It's just that . . . something broke. I'm not your wife any more,' Isabel said, looking into his eyes.

Liudas' throat tightened.

That evening, as always, they stood for a while at the window silently looking down at the late cars whizzing across the bridge, and at how the distorted patterns of neon advertisements reflected in the black water of the river. Cold air blew through the gap in the open window; the breeze was painfully sad but pleasant at the same time.

'I love you,' Liudas said quietly, his eyes focused on the empty road.

'I can feel it,' she said.

In the middle of October Isabel asked him to drive her to Puskai.

LOTS OF SILK IN THE HAIR AND EVERYWHERE

(From a child's note book)

THINGS LOST their brightness last summer. I stood near the well and saw mama in the distance, coming back from Kurpiskiai. She was a pale, watery dot jumping in the disc of light. And suddenly the light that danced upon the grass went out. At first I thought something had happened to mama, but she was still walking towards me and I could see she was smiling.

Something had happened to me.

I lowered my gaze – the grass seemed normal – the blades were flat and neither moved nor shone and it wasn't painful to look at. The bucket by the well looked grey and clear and frozen, as if dead. One of its sides was dented slightly; I had always found this beautiful, but that day it was just a dent.

I never knew that things died.

Nobody told me.

And nobody ever told me that things breathe and shine and that all their tiny parts quiver. Until then it had all seemed so natural. I understood, too, that things hadn't changed; it was I that had changed. Everything shone still, it was just that I could no longer see it.

That was so sad.

Now I could only recall that mama was woven from fibres of silk, from the core of which spread a quivering gentleness. I still quivered when she drew near across the yard and wiped her shoes on the grass. The quiver ran through me when she read the newspaper, bent over the table, occasionally underlining things. I felt it when she opened a can of oil paint and I inhaled the pungent scent.

I had to remember that my mother was made of silk.

Of silk that wasn't ripped or worn.

It was like that worm I accidently cut in half when I was chopping an apple. I was so sad, so unbearably sad that, because of my carelessness, I had cut the chain of life, that I had cut such a complex and perfect circle of life. And I was sad that the world was the kind of place where one person kills another without hesitation. How can you accept this? At that moment I found it horrible; I couldn't accept it. I felt like I was the worm the giant's hand had just cut in half. I felt pain and fear; I was afraid that I was dying. I shouted and squirmed, still able to feel my chopped off tail. It was such burning, screaming pain that it filled my whole body. And it was unbearable and unforgivable that I had caused that suffering – to the worm and to myself. It seemed to me that I would never be able to repair the harm I had done to it, to its children and to the higher being, thanks to which me and the worm had both appeared on the earth. Who could forgive me? Who could make me feel better? Mama was very concerned when I started to cry; she thought it was the start of a seizure, that it was that beast in me which stuck its face out without warning and scared everybody. I live with the beast, but I have never met it. When it sticks its face out, I retreat. I learned about it from mama and my father. The beast has eaten their lives.

I don't see any difference between the worm and myself. Or perhaps just one – that such a small worm couldn't fit a large beast inside it, which means the worm doesn't cause other people pain – while I was born to bring pain. Because of me, mama can't work; she hasn't had enough sleep since I was born. They've never told me this directly, but sometimes they shout at each other with this hatred that I know is actually about me.

When I think about death I can't picture it. I can only feel it as it approaches – it always comes a bit too early. Even if you've tried to get used to it from when you were young it would still be too early. We lack the imaginative leap that would allow us understand it, to really comprehend it. There's always too much life in us. That's why when death makes its first move, when it steps out of the darkness, we won't be expecting it.

I know that my death is growing up with me, and that it is sharp and fast, like a stab. It won't attack me from the back. It will call out with its secret, velvet voice and, when I turn, it will pierce me like a knife. But we will have looked into each other's eyes. It isn't sly – it's just that death is much faster than we are.

And everything in me will relax when death's shroud slithers and shimmers across my skin.

I won't resist.

Because it knows what it is doing.

HOME

ISABEL STOPPED in the yard by the well with her eyes half closed, the colours and the sound of murmuring enfolding her. The ochre October colours seeped through her eye lids, settling in layers, as if they were wrapping her heart in velvet. Overwhelmed, she stood still, breathing and listening. Everything was bright and heavy and saturated with the sad autumnal sun. The bronze fields and the path to Kurpiskiai were spread out before the woods – while in the other direction the burnt beams of the barn looked like a black scrawl. The familiar scent of the dark soil was almost palpable from the depth of the woods. The stream was barely audible, though in a few weeks its serpentine bend would become visible.

She could tell with her eyes closed that autumn had come.

An inexplicable wave of happiness rose abruptly in her chest, freeing itself from its cocoon and rolling out across the fields, throwing itself at the horizon.

She ran around the outside of the house wanting to hug it, to embrace each corner simultaneously. And each log. Out of breath, she sat on the steps of the veranda which were strewn with lilac leaves; those same steps on which Dionisas

Vietusis had played his accordion for the last time more than thirty years before.

When she unlocked the door, the musty scent of the house greeted her like a faithful dog. Isabel took off her jacket, opened wide the windows and walked around the house, the breeze buffeting her, gazing with fresh eyes at the bright, familiar things. The sunlight fell almost imperceptibly across their surfaces.

Her son's things greeted her with lightness and with joy. She could hold them in her hands, she could smell his clothes in the cupboard – the blinding pain had settled into a kind of sadness which it was possible to accept and live with; it had settled into a sadness which she was able to carry in the corners of her heart like a familiar substance. It seemed to Isabel that her child was floating somewhere close, joyfully stretching his hands out towards her from the other side. *I am here, I am still here*, the drawers of the writing table squeaked when she opened them. *You can let me go now*, whispered the drawings of dragons and soldiers that were pinned to the wall. *I need to go*, sighed the fluffed up pillows and the moon.

Fly, fly, I am letting you go. Isabel brushed her hair from her eyes and looked at herself in the mirror above the sideboard. A warm, palpitating shadow unfolded its wings and flew away. She bent closer in order to be sure – the mirror was not steamed up.

She wanted to cry with happiness, she wanted to become completely light, to become weightless, like the strands of light that dominated the house. For a long time she gazed into the eyes of the unfamiliar woman in the mirror.

*   *   *

A slow, quiet life began.

Isabel felt calm; like a person who, having lost everything, finds their heart empty and clear. Time was measured by the shadows which fell away from things, by the rattling of the bucket that cut through the silence, by the sound of the plates and forks being washed – always the same plates with a silver lining and the forks with a pointed handle. Water would heat up, as it always had, on the stove, the third floorboard from the door would squeak, as it always had, in the porch. That year she walked a lot, until the alders stood naked. She walked in the evenings to stand by the river. After dark she would read a book in the kitchen – any childhood book from the attic. Or she would idly move a pencil across an empty piece of paper – and, suddenly, look, a picture – which quivered, and streamed like blood in the veins. Did she eat? Did she sleep? Did she speak? She didn't remember. That indifference of her soul seemed like a kind of fullness. It liberated her from objects and habits so that Isabel didn't remember much from those days. She remembered only the silence, as clear as crystal, touched occasionally by a distant sound. Thoughts, if they came, did not hurt nor disturb her; they rustled more quietly than the wind in the grass and melted away immediately. Days would sail one from another like ripples in the water and everything that touched Isabel quickly poured out of her. When she was asked how she was doing, she could not find the words. She would smile. *I'm fine, thanks*.

This, probably, was happiness.

Soon people started knocking at the door. At first they

knocked shyly, as if she were a stranger, but then more frequently and sincerely.

Pranciska's dog had a litter. One day she brought a soft puppy, as white as a lamb, wrapped in a shawl and placed it carefully on the porch floor. Isabel was worried that she wouldn't be capable of looking after it, or that she wouldn't be able to get used to it, but the pup was serene and unde-manding; it was happy with leftovers and didn't beg for attention.

At first she avoided stroking it and at night she would leave it in the kitchen. But one day she came home from town filled with anxiety and the dog looked at her with such a sense of understanding that Isabel called it to her and talked to it. It smelt like a young, inexperienced hunter, who knew how to listen. It expressed its dog-feelings in a reserved way and had soft, such unbelievably soft fur.

That night he earned himself a name – Nut.

And he was allowed in the big room for the night, next to Isabel's bed.

When she started writing cultural reviews for the daily news-paper, the pace of life picked up, with more noise and events. Isabel started to go into town more often – to the editor's office, to openings of shows and plays. In the car Nut would settle down on the seat next to her and half close his round, brown eyes; sometimes when something sparked his wild nature, he would remind her of a boy she tried to avoid thinking about.

She bought a cheap, old, burgundy Mercedes from a type-setter colleague. At first she regretted it, but the car adjusted to her as Nut had, though it was given neither a name nor the right to spend its nights by her bed. *Well, old man, well,* she would gently tease and encourage it and it would listen to her; and though it coughed and choked, it obeyed her. At dusk she would call Nut and they would speed aimlessly along the roads.

It was enough for them just to head in some direction; the fact that she couldn't think of a purpose for the trip didn't worry her.

The head of the Kurpiskiai primary school offered her a position teaching an art class. It seemed, to her, as if the offer was like a greetings card to which there was no obligation to reply. Isabel shrugged. She observed children from a distance now, like animals you were not allowed to stroke. From afar they looked like joyful, colourful dots – childhood poured not from the noise and the immature shapes but from itself, an ebullient radiance. That radiance unnerved Isabel. She would turn as far away as possible from their forms and voices.

On the first Saturday of November, though, she dreamed of a bright yellow spot on the floor of her father's workshop. She woke up in tears, got up and unlocked the door to the workshop that had stood closed for many years.

A rainy, morning light fell through the window in the roof onto the dusty table. Her father's tools were in boxes along the wall, untouched since the night she had found him in the chair, dead. For fifteen years she hadn't dusted it once – as if doing so would have been as unacceptable as reading somebody else's letter. That night, all dressed up and with lips swollen from kisses, she had called Pranciska and

Juozas for help, and having covered her father with a clean sheet, they moved him still in the chair to the big room. Isabel had gone back to the workroom then, to switch off the light. She locked the door and hid the key in the bottom of the mahogany sideboard.

The workshop table, which was long and wide and took up most of the room, was covered with strips of wood and sketches. A yellowish newspaper lay on one of its corners, and on it – a pencil and an ashtray filled with stubs. On the windowsill she found a plastic comb full of golden hair. *Time calmed these little things*, Isabel thought, *like stones on the riverbed to which you return; you might have changed, but they wait for you the same as they always were, only covered now with the thickening fog of memory*. They testified to events eaten away from recollection and mixed with imagined details, faded in one place and brighter in another. Or possibly they didn't exist at all.

Isabel lifted these objects up, one after another; she found that there were things hidden beneath, stuck together because of length of time they had been lying there, reluctant to separate.

In a cellophane bag there was a folder with some images of a young woman drawn in charcoal. It was the same woman in all of them – with narrow hips, her breasts tiny knots, her eyes, under a high forehead, far away from each other. In some pictures she squatted with her arms around her knees, in others she lay with her knees bent and her arm up in an uncomfortable position, her hair all over her face. Then she sat on the windowsill, sideways, looking, almost, in the opposite direction, her shamelessness mingled with an unhealthy sense of insecurity. It seemed like she was somehow begging for help, begging for her anxieties to be eased.

Isabel hadn't thought of her mother in that way for a long time.

She recognised her from her posture – her mother looked suspicious, her head tilted on one side. And from her bitten lip rippled a mood Isabel was all too familiar with. The expression annoyed Isabel. She was about to put the drawings down, to quash the mixture of emotions which she had carried in the archives of her memory like old, dangerous letters.

But she was too late.

She was caught in a fresh, summer shower. Through the wide open door of the veranda the gusts of rain threw their damp scent inside. Her mother had just come in; water dripped from her long, dark hair and her imitation silk Sunday dress was stuck to her shivering body. Rain dripped rhythmically into the three bowls on the veranda steps. Her mother smiled at somebody only she could see, her eyes closed, beating a barefoot rhythm on the floor, as Isabel tiptoed behind her. They both had thin, sun tanned thighs, bitten by mosquitos and scratched by raspberry bushes. Isabel kept her eyes on her mother's face, from which rose frightening waves of what could only be described as happiness – Isabel was on her guard – if her mother opened her eyes suddenly, she might catch her gaze. Her mother would understand what it was that Isabel wanted to tell her – that she was her daughter and did everything like she did.

And she did not care what other people might think.

Her mother opened her eyes, stretched out her arms to Isabel, and Isabel ran towards the hug. They laughed, drowning out the sound of the rain. Her mother swung her hips, rhythmically; Isabel grew dizzy and allowed herself to close her eyes, just for a moment. She could smell the dampness of her clothes, the camomile cream and, when her mother laughed, loud and birdlike, she could smell something else, too sharp for a child.

Her mother took Isabel into the garden and hugging her hard, ran along the path. The rain splashed against them heavily and the sharp leaves from the apple tree hacked at their skin. Her mother stopped laughing; her chest was rising and falling and Isabel stopped too and looked into her face.

She could feel that something bad was going to happen.

Her mother was hugging her too hard.

Leaving the garden, they turned in the direction of the river; Isabel noticed, over her shoulder, how her father burst from the kitchen window looking in their direction. Isabel grew calmer – her father would drop what he was doing and run after them, he would grab her mother by the hand, would say something to her in his quiet, but firm voice – as if he were talking to a child – and her mother would give Isabel to him.

Her father's hands were strong but gentle – he never squeezed Isabel painfully and if she started squirming he put her down on the floor, she didn't even have to ask.

ON MONDAY Isabel went to the school in Kurpiskiai and asked the head teacher when she could start.

The children were quiet – five girls and two boys. She had been so worried about the first class that she had run all the way from Puskai, holding her skirt, so that her fears would not have time to take root inside her. Instead, she scattered them into the wind behind her.

Isabel stopped in front of the wooden school, out of breath. It was an overcast November day. She could see through the windows that the children had stayed behind in the art classroom waiting for her. They stood around one table talking together in a lively manner – their mouths opening and closing, their heads close together, like little bubbles. When Isabel stamped her feet on the wet doormat and pushed open the door, the children quickly moved to their places.

Seven pairs of eyes fixed upon Isabel. She had forgotten what it was like to have a child scrutinise her. The whites of their eyes were almost blue, like ice, and in the centre their irises glistened warmly, stippled like a quail's egg. All of them. She had also forgotten how their hands were small and bitten by cold, interlocked obediently now on the desks.

'Hello, here I am.' Isabel smiled.

She held the class twice a week at first and in that time the children's gaze began to change, it started to show trust; the icy blue warmed up and their freckled, quail-egg eyes, cracked happily, as if the chicks were hatching.

That autumn seemed to last forever, like a wound that would not heal – as slow as only autumn could be. But gradually the fading copper in the trees coagulated like old blood and one morning frost glittered on the grass.

Isabel managed to negotiate with the headmistress to move her art class to Puskai.

Then suddenly it snowed. It was as if somebody had drawn a sparkling white boundary in the year. It snowed and didn't thaw. Winter had come. The children slid along the path that Isabel had walked so many years before.

They would stay until it grew dark in her father's workshop. Having explained something new, Isabel would give the children an art book to pass round – she had collected lots of them, some in different languages. The small hands, smudged with ink, could barely hold them, they were so heavy. And not just because they were so thick, with hard covers, and as massive as gravestones. They had come from a different, distant world, a world it would have been difficult to believe in if they didn't have the evidence in their hands. Those radiant books swayed in their hands, hesitantly, as if ready at any moment to slip out and escape back to wherever it was they had come from. Though the people in them looked realistic, they led a life that was interesting and different. The light and shadows in the painted faces hid the mystical drama which simple, everyday people didn't suspect that they might have when they trudged across snow bound fields in the dusk carrying bread and vodka, or when, dog-tired, they rested their forehead against the cow's flank while milking. These were people the children knew, these were the houses they had grown up in; the light of their souls penetrated so very faintly through the poverty and the tiredness that you had to learn how to recognise it. These souls-transformed-into-pictures kindled in the children an anxious presentiment that some wonderful meaning was hidden behind the grey routine of work, of eating and sleep. And that significance awaited them somewhere close, beyond the turning of the year, beyond winter, beyond the mended gloves and the constant hunger that they felt in their growing, vitamin deficient bodies.

The children were always hungry. While they painted

Isabel would make a pie from curd, or some sandwiches. They wouldn't hurry home, even after they had eaten everything and discussed everything and their eyes could hardly stay open from tiredness, they would move slowly around the kitchen, irritating each other and leaving paint marks everywhere.

After taking them back to Kurpiskiai, Isabel would be startled by her own steps as she returned across the frosty fields. The creaking of the snow reminded her that she was alive and that her feet touched the ground, but how meaningless it seemed, to come back to a house with only one window lit. The loud ticking of the clock hurt her and the sound of the things she stumbled into was like the short, unhealthy cough of an asthmatic. Place the kettle on the stove, fetch the cup with the forget-me-not pattern, the tinkle of a tea spoon on the sugar bowl. And this repeated several times a day, as if something might be changed by the ritual.

Gailius' room was the quietest. Its silence was a dead nerve in the heart of the house. And that quietness was still too heavy for Isabel. She would leave the door open slightly so that she could get used to the cold light that emanated from his room, and to the contours of the desk that loomed in its depths. When she was cleaning, she would enter that room as well. And while running the sponge over the dim, polished surfaces she would fool herself, for a moment, that it was necessary.

One evening, while her art class were making a noise over their drawings, she switched on the light in Gailius' room and scooped books and toys randomly from the shelves and took them into the kitchen.

From that point on, Gailius' room grew emptier and emptier.

Isabel's heart hurt with every piece of clothing she gave away, as if she were burying her son once more, item by item. But on their new owners the clothes immediately lost their memory, taking root anew and Isabel didn't have to remember how they had been worn by a boy now dead.

Perhaps that was how it was supposed to be.

Like shedding old, ill-fitting skin.

At night Isabel would leave the door unlocked.

She would lie on her bed, having switched off the lamp decorated with flying cranes, and listen. After listening intently for a long while, the frost-locked ground would gift her – the creak of footsteps. She would hold her breath and wait for the squeak of the opening door. But it never happened. The door did not open; only the warm sparks in the stove crackled.

Sometimes she would wake in the night crying, desperately searching for a warm body among the folds of the sheets. The chill on the other side of the bed would sting her hands. She would press cold fingers between her thighs, curl into a ball and pray for somebody breathing, for somebody alive next to her. Nut would come to the bed and lick her ear and smell her face anxiously as if he understood.

On Christmas Eve Isabel answered a couple of telephone calls and, in a voice as joyful as she could manage, refused the invitations. Later, she gazed for a long time at the screen of her mobile where *Liudas'* name shone. She didn't answer.

She didn't cook anything, she didn't prepare anything,

and she didn't think. At dusk she lit the stove, sat on the chair and gazed into the flames. Her cheeks warmed up and her knees burned. When she stood up quickly, her head spun and a heat flamed at the back of her throat.

She swallowed an aspirin and went to bed.

During the night somebody walked quietly around the cottage – she heard the soft crackling of the snow over the throbbing heat at her temples, but she was too weak to lift her head from the pillow. She sank into a scorching sleep and then rose to the surface for a while. She could barely open her heavy eyelids in order to check whether it was still dark. Then she fell asleep again as if pressed down by a hot stone.

Her temperature had dropped by morning. The window was grey with frost. Feeling lighter, her night gown wet with sweat, Isabel turned over and went back to sleep.

She woke feeling bright. She felt like jumping out of bed and opening the curtains so that they fluttered and sang. She ran barefoot to the kitchen to put the kettle on. Outside the window a blinding whiteness hurt her eyes, which were still sensitive from sleep; it had snowed again during the night.

On the even, cottony surface of the snow there were fresh footprints. Isabel felt numb.

From the window she could see clearly that the footprints were those of an adult.

But *he* could have worn shoes too big for him.

She pulled on her fur coat and, barefoot, put on old winter shoes and opened the door to the cold porch.

In the corner there was a bundle wrapped in green and red checked paper. Isabel took it to the kitchen and, with trembling hands, ripped open the package; six large oranges rolled out like juggling balls. At that moment somebody knocked shyly on the door. Isabel ran her hand through her tussled curls, pulled the fur coat tightly around her, hiding the forget-me-nots on her nighty and involuntarily bit her lip – if she had seen herself from the side it would have reminded her of her mother.

Outside, clutching a basket to her coat, stood Mortele Luksyte, Pranciska's niece. Her face was as small as a berry under a woollen hat.

'Merry Christmas,' the girl said, each syllable of the greeting growing quieter and quieter. She handed over food wrapped in cling film.

'Come in,' Isabel invited.

Mortele, who lived with her grandma, was a second year pupil at the school in Kurpiskiai and the most enthusiastic, if not the most gifted artist in Isabel's class. Her mother had once again failed to come to visit her on Christmas Eve. Mortele explained that she expected her to arrive the next day, and her father too – her father had sent her a card from Norway with reindeers on it which played a tune. Mortele furtively opened her fur coat – glitter was falling off the reindeers' horns, the front of her green jumper looked as if it had been decorated. The reindeers were still young and naughty – they had run away, leaving Father Christmas napping in his sledge, with a bag full of presents. They peeped mischievously from their hiding place behind the snowy fir trees. That meant somebody might not receive their Christmas presents, some naughty children like those two reindeers.

Something reindeer-like flashed in Mortele's eyes.

They listened to the music which would begin to play when you opened the card. They drank Kissel with Pranciska's pastries, and then mint tea with the carrot cake Isabel had made. Then they curled up on the double bed with the TV on and watched a Christmas programme. On the screen the snow glittered and some dressed-up, famous people congratulated one another and toasted each other tilting their champagne glasses towards the screen as if offering Isabel and Mortele the chance to take part. Mortele watched their jokes with wide-eyes and a serious face, offering her own imaginary glass clutched tightly in her fist every time the champagne glasses approached the screen.

'Are they drunk?' she asked.

'They're not drinking real champagne,' Isabel explained.

'Like us.'

Soon after the girl rubbed her eyes and fell asleep, her nose tucked into Isabel's shoulder. Isabel moved the girl's head carefully onto the pillow and covered her with her jumper.

Just before four it grew dark, only the green light from the TV danced on the carpet. Isabel brought Mortele an orange – its cold, porous skin stuck to her fingers and made her feel strangely sad. The girl was already awake, her eyes open. She was looking at the ceiling with the dull gaze of a child just woken; there was no sign of any reindeers. Nor of Christmas glitter. Careful not to startle the girl, she put the fruit down next to her. Its strong, Christmassy scent felt almost painful. But Mortele blinked, washing away the cloudy film from her eyes and squeezed the orange. Her palm was tiny, too tiny for such a thing.

They dressed up warmly and whistled for Nut to join them. From under a rug in the porch Isabel pulled out a sledge – its rusty blades left brown marks in the snow. Without telling the girl, she followed the footmarks she had discovered that morning. They took her to the narrow road in the woods and ended by some car tracks.

The woods were tangled in silence. Snow weighed down the branches of the fir trees; they fell to the ground in white and green folds, like curtains. The secret niches of the fir trees, where, when the snow melted, a warm green light would shine and the birds would make nests, were empty.

They turned off the road and headed deep into the thick woods. Nut barked crazily in the painfully clear air and their steps and half whispered words bounced from the snow.

Blood pounded noisily at Isabel's temples. Hot and bright. If she turned her head suddenly, red circles spread before her eyes.

They stopped, tired. The noise stilled; the silence of the woods buzzed in their temples.

'Look,' the girl said.

While Isabel had stood quietly, as if asleep with her eyes open, the girl had made a burrow in the snow and, lying down, had curled up in it. Only her head stuck out of the burrow with a strand of dark hair sticking out of the cap and her eyes were as blue as blueberries, set too close to each other.

'I've made a house.'

Isabel made a similar one under another tree.

The snow was warm and friendly, like a living body, but formed of a different material. When touched, it would mould into shapes, like angels – which she could feel rather than see.

The snow breathed. It glowed in the dark like phosphorous over the bones of the dead.

Isabel lay in the snow cocoon with only her head and shoulders out; she felt the snow's cool hardness against her cheek. The world above her was like a Christmas card tilted on its side.

Then silently, like an unexpected greeting, the occasional large snowflake began to fall from the sky. Settling on her forehead, her eyes and lips.

'Oh, you have a house too,' the girl giggled from her burrow.

EARLY IN spring a new photographer joined the editorial team; a fair haired student who wore a stylish leather cap and had a feminine nose, with sensual nostrils which flared when he spoke. His eyebrows, though, were masculine, as was his high, intelligent forehead. His habit of turning his sharp gaze on the strangest aspects of the world had given his features a maturity beyond his years. He looked like the kind of serious student that listened to his lecturers' advice and was restrained in his ridicule of authority. He valued style. Because he was creatively searching for his own style, he constantly scrutinised other people's faces, their postures and moods, in what seemed like a slightly arrogantly manner. He had been taught to always be on the lookout for 'characters' and to capture them in an original way.

He would settle at the back of the weekly meetings in the editorial office, by the window, so that he could flash Isabel brief, sharp, whip-like glances. When it was Isabel's turn to speak, he would turn and focus his attention on her face with the intensity of a dog sniffing at the ground, barely able to hide his excitement.

Karolis Galcikas, nostrils flaring, brought her coffee on a couple of occasions while she was editing her articles at the typesetter's computer. The first time was the 23rd of March – she remembered it as clearly as if it had been the day before – he had placed the cup on the table and Isabel had thanked him without lifting her eyes. The second time, a week later, he put the cup of coffee directly into her hands, as if it were some kind of coded love letter. His fingers trembled slightly. Sensing something, she glanced up absent-mindedly and smiled.

Sometime later they had coffee together in the café downstairs. They even had lunch together, though it was difficult to shake off their colleagues.

As time passed Karolis managed to attract longer and more personal glances from Isabel, though, in fact, the look she gave him was no different to that which she flashed the young waitress who everybody liked because she always knew what people wanted for lunch. The waitress had complained once about how weak her immune system was.

'You could do with drinking freshly pressed grapefruit juice,' Isabel told her, eyeing the snuffling girl carefully.

Karolis, at that moment, was so envious of the attention Isabel gave to the girl that he even began sniffling himself. And then he blushed.

At the beginning of April he plucked up the courage to ask Isabel if she would model for him. He had to prepare something for his exam, he explained, and Isabel's unusual and subtle features would really suit the idea he had. He wanted her portrait, he quickly clarified. And then he almost blushed again. Isabel wasn't surprised – she raised her eyebrows as if chasing a thought that had escaped her – she was in the middle of editing an article.

She agreed to be photographed. First they dropped into a café to have something warm to drink. In the street the snow was thawing quickly. Occasionally the sun shone brightly, but then it hid behind the thick spring clouds. Karolis' fingers trembled so much he was reluctant to touch his camera. Stirring lemon and honey into her tea, Isabel lifted her gaze to his high-cheeked, flawless face. The peak of his leather cap cast a shadow over his anxious, melancholy blue eyes. And suddenly Isabel understood.

'Your hands are trembling,' she said softly.

'Yes,' Karolis answered in a whisper.

'I'm thirty two. I've lost everything that I had managed to build up over the years. I'm afraid to start anything new,' Isabel said after a pause.

'Isn't it too early to make such assumptions?'

She didn't answer. For a long time, as if mesmerised, she stirred the tea until it turned yellow from the lemon juice.

'Anyway, I wasn't expecting anything,' Karolis murmured.

She carried on stirring her tea. Then the tea spoon clinked and stopped.

'Well, maybe I was expecting . . . But – I'm not asking for anything,' Karolis corrected himself.

He managed to steady his hands. The conversation had cleared the air; it explained the trembling and brought his intentions out into the open.

It was Isabel who now began to shake.

'You see, we won't get anywhere today,' she said hiding her trembling fingers. She smiled widely – it was a shame Karolis wasn't able to press the camera's shutter button.

The next day Isabel borrowed some money from a colleague and bought some canvases and oil paints. It was Thursday evening and the snow had nearly melted. The pull of the earth was strong, almost over-powering, but Isabel felt as light as one of the natural bristles on her new paintbrushes. On Fridays she was usually not missed in the office so a long weekend awaited her. She whistled all the way home to Puskai, trying to calm the energy that pulsed impatiently from her fingertips, begging it not to be in a hurry. With a joyful hiss the car splashed through the snow.

She took all the lamps into the workshop, stretched a canvas and took one of the brushes.

She was still painting at dawn.

From the canvas poured a chaotic mantle of blood and diamonds. In its whirls flashed barely discernible human foetuses – or perhaps souls, thickening and searching for a form, cracked like precious stones, pierced by lightning and separated from each other by strange arabesques of plants and mythical animals. Here was the eye of a unicorn – glittering planets flew within it at incredible speeds. And here, in swelling space, a bloody horn which a brown-eyed angel blew like a trumpet of war, while peeling off the devil's skin.

Isabel leant back; she was short of breath, as if she had just read her own secret story.

She stretched a new canvas on the easel; daubed some strokes on it but suddenly felt tired. She made some coffee and, having dipped an old hard bun in warm milk, she swallowed it in few bites. A gloomy Friday morning was breaking outside the window. In the distance Pranciska, wrapped in a shawl with roses on it, tottered across the fields which were loud with the song of the larks. Her eldest daughter, Jadviga, had been running the shop for a number of years, but when her health permitted, Pranciska, moved energetically between the boxes of bread and flour, chased out flies and talked to the customers every day until lunch. Many of the customers had dropped in specifically to talk to her. But on those days when God didn't grant her health, Pranciska would slump in the chair next to the fridge with the ice cream and drinks (*every village shop had one of those fridges with glass windows* – she would say with surprise), observing eagerly who bought what and keeping an eye on how much change they received.

Isabel drew the kitchen curtains and returned to the workshop.

By lunch the clouds had begun to clear and a blot of sun blossomed on the canvas which smelled strongly of paint. Isabel laughed; a short, sharp laugh, like the stroke of a paint brush. Then suddenly she felt that there was somebody at the window.

Instinctively she lifted her head and behind the glass saw a pair of eyes.

Not brown. Intensely blue.

He didn't wear a cap to mask his anxiety.

He met Isabel's surprised gaze and his attractive nostrils quivered. He managed to hold her look and his cheeks remained as pale and hard as marble.

Recovering herself, Isabel put down the brush and unlocked the door to the garden. Karolis turned to her, putting a smouldering cigarette to his lips. Next to him his dirty bike rested against the wall.

'How did you find me?' Isabel asked.

He didn't answer. He examined her face as if attempting to gauge whether she was unhappy about his sudden appearance, and then once again he drew hungrily on his cigarette.

'Come in,' she said.

She left the door open.

They made love until Saturday evening, with short breaks for food and drink. Even then their fingers searched for each other's as if they were iron and magnet, or strands of hair wound into a single plait. They jumped on each other with the last bite of food still in their mouths, or having met in the doorway – rip off what couldn't be ripped off, eager to give something it wasn't possible to give.

His body was young but strong and virile – more mature than his eyes, which lost in those hours their arrogance and knowingness. Yes, he knew how to touch and satisfy her, though he wasn't aware of that himself. His nature unfolded, sensitive and sensual, slightly feminine; tangled in the sparkling white sheets he looked vulnerable and at the same time frighteningly strong. Tired, they embraced, wrapping their legs and fingers around each other, sprawled like two single strands of fabric, silently scrutinising each other, for a short moment sinking back inside themselves as if plumbing the depths for some kind of an explanation. Or they talked, lazily, their voices tired. They talked about themselves, lifting from the dark depths fragments of their essence and bringing them up to the light in words. They spoke and listened to each other. Until they were struck once more by desire, sparked by a movement or a glance; it would tense their muscles, glue their bodies together and create from them innumerable shapes.

On Saturday, at dusk, Isabel lifted her sleeping lover's arm from her chest and locked herself in the workshop.

He knocked after midnight. He stood in the doorway naked, ruffled, his eyes half closed, squinting in the bright light of the lamps, and from him the decaying smell of their relationship diffused, like from a bouquet of withering flowers. He snuggled against her, searching for her lips, desperate to carry on as they had the previous night. But no feeling of desire stirred in Isabel.

Karolis went to bed alone and slept through until midday on Sunday.

Later they drank coffee in silence. Over the rims of their cups they exchanged long, intimate glances. In the morning light Karolis looked unforgivably young and slightly sour, but a single cheerful glance from Isabel would brighten his features. He waited for Isabel to suggest that they should meet up again, but the only thing she could think about was the three canvases drying in the workshop. She felt both an uncontrollable desire and at the same time an intense fear that the drawings would have changed or would look different to the way they had at night. She attempted to explain this to Karolis, but talking about other things hurt him. Isabel stopped talking and turned to the window.

'When will we see each other again?' Karolis asked with studied indifference.

'I don't know, at the office.'

'That's not what I had in mind.'

'I'll call you.'

'Sure?'

'Yes, of course.'

Isabel was not sure, but 'yes' sounded nicer than 'no'.

She walked with Karolis up to the woods. His bike rattled by his side like the keys to the heart. On the narrow road they looked at each other and hugged, suddenly, the former attraction and heat rising in them, their lips opening for a long kiss that delighted the mind. Then he walked away along the road, pushing his rattling bike, pressed in by the fir trees. His light hair fluttered, a drop of gold drawing into the distance. And as he disappeared into the depths of the wood, her eyes followed him and Isabel realised that she missed and would always miss what one person could never give to another; it was something they could only awaken and fuel.

The canvases were waiting for Isabel, luring her with the aroma of a spell. She, though, was afraid to walk through the doorway and look at them.

She stood in the yard for a long time gazing out across to the woods, across the garden with its apple trees, which were as knobbly as arthritic fingers, and at the fields on the Kurpiskiai side, that were shyly flushed with green.

Later she wandered in the woods; they were damp and smelled of earth. She crossed the road and found herself in the alder woods where bright, sharp leaves were forcing themselves out from buds, their thin cuticles sparkling in the sunlight creating an aura of thickening green light.

She walked for a long time among the pale trunks, which were finely dotted like the feathers of a thrush and stretched so tightly that it looked as if they were about to burst from the tension. It grew hot; she took off her jumper and tied it around her waist. A sticky, spring wind bit into her bare chest.

A small lake flashed among the tree trunks.

The lake lay quietly in the depths of the forest, as round as a polished precious stone. Emerging from the trees it would be possible to stumble upon it unexpectedly and on a sunny day the light on the water would be blinding.

Isabel stopped at the water's edge and inhaled its sun-glittering blueness.

At that moment the water was disturbed and small waves broke on the bank. A grey head appeared in among the rushes. Isabel let out a silent gasp, then, realising it was a grey haired woman, she stepped back into the shade of the bushes.

The woman climbed out of the water. Droplets sparkled like scales on her naked, bony body. Isabel felt as if she were looking at herself. As if a hidden part of herself had stepped out of water – famished, with small sagging breasts, mobile, jutting hipbones like cogwheels, a dripping knot of grey hair at the back of her head and skin wrinkled like crumpled paper. Yet still full of a frightening, vital force.

Without noticing Isabel who was hidden in the dense undergrowth, the grey haired woman began putting clothes on her wet body.

Isabel could bear it no longer.

She turned round and started to run, struggling through the wet moss and horror.

She ran until she reached the road.

In the fir woods everything was familiar and she attempted to slow down. To resign herself to eternally walking in the woods. With every moment her skin grew looser and began falling away from her bones, wrinkled, like a cape slipping off. The boy who had flashed like lightning between her sheets did not exist at all – she had only taken him into her bed because he reminded her of somebody long lost. The sheet in the big room was crumpled and scented only with her longing and her inability to stand the deafening silence which was interrupted only by the squeak of the door she opened.

The following week she didn't raise her eyes to meet Karolis' gaze.

And he seemed to accept Isabel's mute distance.

He didn't do anything drastic; he didn't demonstrate his determination. Occasionally he appeared behind her unexpectedly, as if he was waiting for a sign, as if he was trying to transmit his thoughts to her. Isabel didn't listen. Again and again she climbed out of the lake which never grew warm, feeling as lonely and as aged as the knobbly branch of an apple tree.

OVER THE next four year more canvases emerged. Isabel was consumed by a tireless, playful spirit; it rioted and poured out through her hand. At first she had to borrow money for the canvases and paint. Then buyers appeared. An elderly Lithuanian from Chicago, Benecijus Krincius, bought three painting at once. He wore rubber boots and a waterproof coat and in his search for her farmhouse had prepared himself as if he were going on an expedition. He paid so much for the paintings that the cottage in Puskai got running water and Isabel installed an internet connection and fixed the roof. She was free, now, not just from ever having to borrow money, but it allowed her to write articles only when she wanted to.

In addition, Benecijus put Isabel in touch with a few more wealthy clients. In Puskai Benecijus felt he was Columbus discovering America. It wasn't hard to guess that it wasn't just the gloomy nature and the art that attracted him to Puskai, but, among other things, the hostess herself who fluttered like the flame in an oil lamp. He wrote her long, intellectually sensual letters. He would arrive wearing a bright, white suit, like a peace offering, and from a distance his smile would shine as luminously as his outfit. He openly begged her to paint his portrait and indirectly too; he was ready to buy a cat in the sack as long as it was painted by Isabel.

At first, Isabel wasn't interested in the idea of painting portraits. And not just of Benecijus.

But then one spring she met Beatrice in town.

The afternoon was stuffy; Beatrice wore a strapped dress with Egyptian hieroglyphs on it. At her sides, like two sphynxes, stood her sons, who had grown bigger and were dark like her. Isabel had heard that Beatrice had left her position as the headmistress of the orphanage, had separated from Eimuntas Brasiskis and gone to find happiness in

London. It was difficult to tell whether she had found it. She had barely changed, though possibly she looked slightly more worn, but that might have been just that she had forgotten to apply red lipstick to her full, quirky lips. They stood at a polite distance from each other, hiding their embarrassment and smiled into the space between them.

The conversation that followed was muddled, with uncomfortable pauses. Beatrice's bored guards kicked around and grumbled. Isabel was not keen to talk about herself or listen to Beatrice's news. But a brown eyed boy flashed in the space between them like a bat.

'Well, we have to get a move on. Let's meet up some day for a glass of wine and a chat,' Beatrice said at the end of another long pause.

'Call me when you're free,' Isabel agreed.

'By the way, did you hear that Ilya ran away? It's been about six month now with no news. Vaidotas Zulonas is in my place now. He's such a conformist . . . do you remember? Even at university he knew whose shoes to lick . . . I'm sure he couldn't care less about the child. He could find him if he looked. But he doesn't care.'

On her way back along the sun dappled road to Puskai, Isabel already knew that she would paint a portrait. She would paint Benecijus. She would paint freely, not from a model but from memory and with a friendly touch of irony.

However, after a couple of hours in the workshop, two piercing brown eyes shot out at her from the canvas. Isabel leant back, surprised and frightened, but her hand cared nothing about her emotions and continued to slap against the canvas, mercilessly spreading the familiar features.

She finished as dusk fell. From the bloody twilight the confused yellow face of a boy stared out at her. His lips were pressed tightly together, his forehead thrust forward like a lamb's, a shy plea for help lingered hauntingly in the depths of his eyes.

Isabel turned the canvas towards the wall and went out into the yard.

She felt short of breath. In the darkness, soft gusts of wind ruffled the leaves of the apple trees and then sank into silence. There, the pattern of the breathing trees converged in a black ball – Isabel went down the veranda steps and plunged into them. It was cool and damp there, the bark of the fruit trees whispered incoherently, with a caressing, motherly shushing. She felt everything so sharply and deeply – the uncut grass tangled like wet hair around her calves, a veil of cool air drew over Isabel, dew trickled through her hair. Above the apple trees bats shuttled silently like black maple leaves; at the bottom of the garden the spring gurgled and the nightingale, its trill a silver needle, stitched the darkness. All this nestled up against Isabel, talked to her, blessed her. She, too, radiated warmth and sound and caressed the night with her breathing; she was woven of that same cloth. But a human weariness and a sense of disappointment prevented her from uniting with it fully, from believing in her transparency . . . *I am too heavy*, Isabel whispered, leaning against the rough trunk of an apple tree. *What happened to me?*

A silhouette moved slightly among the furthest apple trees, as if hiding behind the fork of one of the trunks; the shape was warmer and more lithe than the trunks of the fruit trees. Isabel stopped. The grass was silent; the leaves on the apple trees said nothing. *It* stuck to the bark of the tree like a second skin. In the thick dusk it was impossible to tell – it could just have been a knot in the tree, an inanimate shape distorted by the night.

'Ilya?' Isabel shouted.

Only the wind ran through the leaves of the apple trees. The forked tree stood motionless, nobody moved from it, nor made a sound, nor answered. Isabel turned and flew quickly back into the veranda, listening to whether someone was following her. The darkness breathed down her neck loudly. Disconcerted, she slammed the door closed, as if she were never going to open it again. She checked, then, the other two doors, and shouted for Nut who was half asleep. Gingerly she approached the window – as if it were infected – and drew the blinds.

Before going to bed she put a bread knife next to her pillow.

In the morning she pulled herself together and called Liudas.

Over the four years they had seen each other occasionally.

'We need to talk. If you're in town shall we go for a coffee?'

Whenever Isabel agreed to have a coffee with Liudas she liked to go somewhere on the main street in town; somewhere so noisy they could barely hear each other speak. They could look around, watch people, drop a purse or a teaspoon under the table and then look for it for a long time – anything so that they didn't have to look at each other. There had been a couple of times when Isabel had gone into town mainly for coffee with Liudas, having pretended she had business there.

Each time Liudas would repeat the same offer – to take a last minute cheap holiday. He would try to convince her that as the 'Liudvikas' agency was thriving, Isabel could choose any country she wanted and Liudas would pay for it. He would, in fact, pay for something more expensive. If she was short of money. He promised her two tickets but never offered to accompany her. The other ticket was meant for somebody Isabel might want to go with. Her girlfriend or a man – Liudas' eyes would narrow, attempting to read in Isabel's face whether she had somebody for the other ticket. Isabel, though, would only shake her head stubbornly. She would come up with an excuse like she couldn't leave the house empty, as if she could hear from a distance how dusty it would get. When she imagined climbing onto the plane – she hated planes – a terrible chill would freeze her heart, as though somebody was tightening an invisible umbilical cord that bound Isabel to her home. In other words, she spoke and behaved in the same way she had always done, the style which had attracted Liudas so much at first and then pushed him away. The style which made his fingers tremble now, when he bent to pick up Isabel's tea spoon from the floor. Above the table, two glittering, damp eyes waited for him in the café where the noise made everything seem less intimate. *I could have picked it up myself. Don't do that next time,* their owner reproached him. And the same dampness would appear suddenly in Liudas' eyes as well.

And unconsciously she would also try to read – from his clothes, from his barely changed manners and his scent which at times was so familiar, but sometimes scared her with its newness – whether Liudas had somebody else for the other ticket. Or at least for a double bed. But even if there was a woman circling him – and he was that type of man that women *circled* – Liudas probably wouldn't have taken her on a trip. Why was Isabel so certain about that? Maybe because there still flashed the old anchor of gentleness and care in his eyes. That, though, didn't guarantee that Isabel was still the only woman Liudas looked at.

Like two animals they would meet to sniff each other, to make sure that they were still the same, that they could still read each other, that the old, redundant intimacy still smouldered in them. And then they parted, having checked each other out, or marked each other, though they didn't think about it that way. They never invited each other to their homes. Isabel knew only that Liudas had moved again and lived now somewhere in the Old Town. He had three rooms with windows looking out onto Bekesh mountain. Liudas hadn't been back to Puskai since Isabel had set the barn on fire.

So that morning, having woken up with the bread knife at her side, the sun playing on its blade, Isabel called Liudas, barely able to control her excitement.

For a long time he didn't answer. Finally she heard a quiet *Hello* at the other end of the line.

'I need to leave.' The words sprang from her easily.

'Isabel, is that you?'

'To the mountains. Get me a trip to the mountains.'

THE IDEA of the trip washed through her in an uncontrollable, long-awaited, unstoppable wave. There was a burden deep in Isabel's heart which for years had been hidden from the sunlight, growing beneath the dark, cool sheets, incubated like some kind of disastrous egg. Compared with that baggage, the travel bag into which she threw some underwear, some warm clothes, a toothbrush and a hair brush seemed incredibly light. The bag was only to distract inquisitive eyes; Isabel could travel without it in fact. She couldn't find her mirror – the kind of round powder mirror women take on trips – anywhere. Perhaps she had broken it, or had thrown it away when everybody had left her so suddenly. For years it had been difficult for her to have a face, to push herself, day in, day out, like some kind of meaningless monument, to suffer the thoughts that ruthlessly tore at her mind leaving wounds that would not heal. Or worse, to pretend those thoughts didn't bother her and that therefore she was happy. She had shattered her brain so that it no longer reflected the events that had happened long ago and so that the lost faces didn't shout at her in the night, bending over her bed like over a well in the cemetery. She had smashed the mirrors and had forgotten everything, though she hadn't forgiven anybody, and that deliberate annihilation of the past didn't mean that it disappeared, it just grew sourer and the large, dark lump grew in her gut.

She took it all with her, everything that had been growing inside her, everything that had been accumulating in her for years, as much as she was able to carry. She took the light of the sunset in the doorway of the barn, the twilight in the ferns, the wound in the stomach that had opened again on the way to the city. All those endless days when she had stood slowly dying before the shirt of her son, in front of his pencils left in the shape of a cross, the ball of modelling clay, trying to explain and to justify to herself the injustice, to put everything back together again. All those nights when she had listened to the other-worldly sounds, when she was afraid and hated, when she had killed in her mind and then resurrected from the dead.

She had never been to the mountains but longed for them as if knowing that their hostile nature would be cleansing; she longed for their pure, welcoming emptiness in which the most hardened knots in her heart could be unravelled and melt away.

She sped along the road – that road which headed into town as straight and cold as the blade of a knife. Isabel felt a new lightness as she drove, as if it were the last time she would pass along that road, and it was true, she didn't know if she ever would again. *I am getting lighter*, she thought. And then, almost losing control on a sharp bend, she laughed – *I am light!*

The plane was due to leave early the next morning. Isabel had arranged to stay overnight at her friend's house and leave her car there.

It was getting dark; in the city the street lights were on. Turning at the train station Isabel thought: *I will never do the same thing twice again.* She was not quite sure what this might mean, but these thoughts that came to her raised her spirits.

She left her car in the car park and went to exchange some money for the next day's journey. The queue was long but moved fast.

It felt quite natural to be among people, but she was a

little distant, as if in a dream. She didn't feel anxious or have a desperate need to leave immediately. The bank clerk looked tired but pleasant; Isabel felt the warmth of her fingers on the banknotes.

In the street something annoyed her. It was dark and the street light shone in a melancholy manner above the trolleybus stop. Next to her Mercedes there was a dark shadow – when she looked more carefully she saw that it was a man, a young man wearing a black cap and carrying a bucket in his hand. It was easy to see, even from a distance, that he was begging.

'Missus, give me some money, I washed your car,' the boy said motioning with his hand.

She didn't recognise his voice, she couldn't have recognised it; it had been so long ago.

But suddenly something rippled through Isabel, scorched her like electricity – they were both startled, their eyes locking onto each other.

Only his eyes were still the same – the rest was distorted, stretched out, as if re-made. Those features that had been closed up blossomed now, acquiring a vicious brightness and a terrible, ghastly beauty.

They leapt away from each, repulsed like two magnets. Isabel slid inside her car and slammed the door. She sat there for a moment with her eyes lowered and felt a shiver run through her body, sensing, still, through the glass *that child*.

He stood there, a dark smudge with a slightly lighter face. Only the glass separated them. There had always been something to separate them.

He stood there like stranger. He wasn't afraid, he didn't run away. He only needed a coin from Isabel.

Isabel fished some money from the pocket of her jacket and reached out to him. From the darkness a greedy hand grasped at the coins; Isabel jumped as her fingers brushed against his clammy palm. In her mind's eye the blade of a knife flashed with lightning speed. Only the coins flashed now, flashed and fell from her hand, disappearing into Ilya's dark shadow. He didn't thank her, as if he was afraid to let her hear his adolescent voice. Taking his plastic bucket and soapy water into the hostile darkness of the station car park, as if he was afraid of anything that might reveal himself to her, he hurried to his accomplices, a nocturnal hunting pack, who lurked further away among the cars with their buckets.

Ilya exchanged a couple of words with the group and then broke away from them. He walked toward the kiosks. He didn't turn once to see if she had left. Isabel watched his cap as it moved among the crowd, straining to see as he moved away.

Suddenly she was flooded with a feeling of gentleness, a gentleness that had no explanation or reason; a wave that liberated and set right her feelings. Something which came from the earth; from the light; from the ferns; from the depth of the womb; something which was always right and never fully exposed. The lope of the boy as he walked away struck her loins as if, fifteen years before, his head had pushed out into the world from between her thighs.

It reminded her of that feeling of *newness* she had felt driving along the road.

A groan rose from deep inside Isabel, from the very core of her being, as if she were pulling out the mouldy, moth-eaten sheets of her heart. Her heart moved, contracted, as if resisting, squirming before ripping – but she knew that she would be able to do it.

A clean, empty space was opening up behind the glass, a space cut open by the sun.

The mountains were right there.